# THE ADVENTURESS

# THE ADVENTURESS

## Marion Chesney

*A Lythway Book*

CHIVERS PRESS
BATH

First published in Great Britain 1989
by
Firecrest Publishing Limited
This Large Print edition published by
Chivers Press
by arrangement with
the author
1989

ISBN 0 7451 1001 0

British Library Cataloguing in Publication Data available

N, A.

For David and Alice Lynne McKee
and their daughter, Kelly.

# THE ADVENTURESS

# Chapter One

*Oh, her lamps of a night! her rich gold-smiths, print-shops, toy-shops, mercers, hardware-men, pastry-cooks, St. Paul's Churchyard, the Strand. Exeter Change, Charing Cross, with a man upon a black horse! These are thy gods, O London!*

—Charles Lamb

Although darkness still fell early across the neat streets and squares of London's West End, although fog hung in smoky wreaths around the dingy globes of the parish lamps, and not one leaf was to be seen on the trees in Hyde Park, there was an undercurrent of excitement, a rustling, not of leaves, but of taffetas and silks being pinned and fitted. Delicately scented silk blossoms burst out everywhere. That artificial spring, that preparation for the London Season, was making the blood quicken.

Grimy windowsills were being scrubbed white again, shutters were being thrown open to air the rooms, and many members of society grimly prepared for the agonising ritual of their twice-yearly bath.

All the toys of the Season were being brought out of their boxes—the paints and powders and pomatums, the jewels and fans and enamelled snuff boxes. Who in their right mind would dream of wasting such sweet treasures on the rustic air? Huge cumbersome travelling carriages bearing their weight of aristocratic passengers rolled into Town, as the members of the bon ton, heartily weary of their country estates and of keeping up a façade of clean living to set an example to their tenants, figuratively loosened their stays and looked forward to an orgy of balls and routs and parties.

Débutantes knew they were being put on the market for sale, and very few saw anything odd or cruel about that. It was the way of the world. They could only pray that *he* would not turn out to be too old or too ugly. But, in the end, any man would do, for to return unwed after an expensive Season was showing ingratitude to God, who had seen fit to place these young ladies in such an exalted station.

After all, one could have been born to live underground, as one third of the population did, to sweat out one's days as a servant in some basement or other.

But there were servants and servants. Some were lucky. They wintered in great palaces or mansions in the country and then travelled with their masters and mistresses to a well-appointed town house for the Season. They were well-fed and saved from the uncertainties of life.

But for the servants of a certain town house at 67 Clarges Street, every Season was a lottery. Their master, the Duke of Pelham, was barely aware of the existence of this piece of property, for he owned a large mansion in Grosvenor Square. The house in Clarges Street was, therefore, advertised before each Season as being to let. A good tenant meant tips for the servants and, with luck, an increase in their meagre wages, for the letting of the house was handled by the duke's agent, Jonas Palmer, who paid the servants miserable wages, charged his master higher ones, and pocketed the difference.

Times were hard, jobs were scarce, and the small staff of Number 67 had to put up with the bullying and odious Palmer. The butler, Mr. John Rainbird, and the footman, Joseph, had been dismissed from previous jobs for indiscretions which Palmer threatened to broadcast to the world should either show signs of escaping to another master. The rest were tied to the house out of loyalty to their butler, and because it would be nigh impossible to find other work without references, and Palmer would certainly not give any of them a good reference should they wish to leave.

The house had been damned as unlucky, not only because the present duke's father had hanged himself there, but due to a subsequent series of dramatic happenings. It was a superstitious age. Each year the servants could only hope that someone outside the circle of London gossip, who had not heard of the bad luck of the house, might be tempted to take it. It was offered at a low rent, only eighty pounds, a fortune to some, but little to the aristocracy, who often paid over one thousand pounds for more inferior accommodation.

But the uncertainty, the hard life, and the long boredom of the winters, which had been unusually severe of late, had bound the servants into a tight-knit family. Apart from Rainbird, the butler, and Joseph, the footman, there was a housekeeper, Mrs. Middleton; a cook, Angus MacGregor; a house maid, Alice; a chambermaid, Jenny; a scullery maid, Lizzie; and a little pot boy called Dave.

They had spent a cheese-paring sort of winter, not because they did not have any money, for they had managed to accumulate quite a sum from the previous tenants, but because they all planned to club together and buy a pub. That way, they could escape from Palmer, escape from the servant class, and be free to marry—for servants were not allowed to marry.

They had all been introduced to the joys of education by a previous tenant and had kept up their studies during the winter. But although their increased knowledge had broadened their interests and raised their conversation above mere gossip, it had also caused a certain amount of restlessness. Not one of them was content with the role of servant. The dream of the pub was so near, and yet, at the same time, so very far away. Rainbird had said they would need another two good Seasons before they could make their escape.

On one chilly day when the morning's frost still glittered unmelted on the street outside, the staff gathered round the table in the servants' hall for their breakfast and to talk again about the hideous disappointment of the day before.

For Jonas Palmer had turned up with a very fine gentleman, none other than the Earl of Fleetwood. The earl was very grand, very rich, and very autocratic. Palmer had not forewarned the servants of the visit, and so the house was cold and the furniture still shrouded under holland covers.

The earl had marched from one room to the other. It did not take him very long. It was a tall, thin house, with two rooms to a floor. The ground consisted of front and back parlours, the first of a dining-room on the front and a bedroom at the back, the second of two bedrooms. The attics at the top housed the servants, with the exception of Mrs. Middleton, who slept in her parlour off the backstairs; Lizzie, the scullery maid, who camped out in the scullery; and Dave, the pot boy, who bedded down under the kitchen table.

Alice, the beautiful and languorous housemaid, said she thought the earl was ever so handsome, but Mrs. Middleton was of the opinion that he looked too clever to be handsome. The earl had thick black hair, a thin face with high cheek-bones that gave him an almost Slav appearance, as did his bright blue eyes, which had a black rim round the pupil and a slight slant at the outside edge. He was tall and well-built and immaculately armoured against the world in Weston's tailoring, sparkling Hessian boots, and one of the most intricately tied cravats the servants had ever seen. But they had all been well-disposed towards him until, after his tour of inspection, he had said with a lazy drawl, "Too poky by half, Palmer. Not at all suitable. Cold as charity in here. I shall need to find somewhere else." And without even a nod towards the listening servants, he had taken himself off.

Now disappointment united them in damning him. Even Dave, who had been considered of too low an order to be present (and because Palmer was unaware of the boy's existence in the household, Rainbird having rescued Dave from a miserable career as a chimney-sweep's boy), had managed to catch a glimpse of the earl as he had left by peeping through the railings at the top of the area steps, and declared him to be "as cold-looking as last week's cod."

"We don't want his sort here," said Joseph, the effeminate footman. "Eh was speaking to Luke and he told me all sorts of things." Luke was first footman at Lord Charteris' town house next door.

"Like whit?" demanded Angus Mac-Gregor, the Scotch cook.

"Lahk he was married and he beat his poor wife to death," said Joseph.

"My stars!" cried Mrs. Middleton, her faded timid face reddening with shock. "When was that?"

"Eight years ago," said Joseph, his genteel accents slipping as he lifted The Moocher, the kitchen cat, down from his lap, leaned his elbows on the table, and prepared to gossip for all he was worth.

"He had only been married a short bit," said Joseph, "when they was down at their place in Sussex. His lady had gone out walking in the wood near the house on the estate wiff 'er little dog. The servants 'eard terrible cries and smashing sounds coming from the wood, and 'er dog, he run home all on 'is lone. They rushed interrawood and found 'er, all blood and battered, she were. 'Orrible, it was.'

"Well, how did they come to think his lordship had done it?" asked Rainbird cynically.

"Afore she died," said Joseph, "she turned 'er beautiful blue eyes up to the

8

heavens and murmured 'Peter.' That's the earl's Christian name, swelp me if it ain't."

"Then why wasn't the earl put in the Tower?" asked Lizzie.

Joseph looked at her haughtily. He still expected Lizzie to hang on his every word, although the girl's uncritical devotion to him seemed to have somewhat faded of late. He rummaged around his vocal chords for his genteel accent.

"Because," he said haughtily, "he's a member of the aristocracy, *thet's* why. They cen get away with anything they lahk. Besides, Luke says as how the earl was out hunting somewhere else."

"So he couldn't have done it," snapped Jenny, the chambermaid, who had little time for Luke.

"But it was a derk day and no one had seen him on the hunting field for some time," said Joseph triumphantly. "They hadn't enough evidence to heng him, but everyone knows he did it, says Luke."

Rainbird glanced at Mrs. Middleton's stricken face. The tale of the murder had made her look quite faint.

"I have never known Luke tell anything other than a pack of lies," he said roundly.

There came a growling, roaring noise that shook the house.

"What's that?" cried Jenny. "Thunder?"

"No," said Rainbird. "Coal. It's so long since we've heard the sound of any being delivered, you've forgotten what the noise is like. Joseph, go up to the pavement and make sure the coal-hole cover is back on. Palmer wants us to light fires in every room, so at least we'll be warm at his expense."

Joseph stalked off, his back stiff with outrage. He obviously thought checking coal-hole covers was beneath him.

Lizzie rested her pointed chin on her hands and looked at the butler with wide pansy-brown eyes. "You know, Mr. Rainbird," she said, "I thought the earl was a fine-looking gentleman. I took a dislike to him because of disappointment and all, but I can't believe Luke's story. I thought Lord Fleetwood looked *kind*."

"But he was so contemptuous," said Jenny. "And he never even looked at us. It was as if we didn't exist."

"Well, we don't," said Rainbird reasonably, "not as far as the aristocracy is concerned. We've been spoiled by some unusual tenants. Hey ho! Lackaday! Why don't you send us down a tenant, O Lord!"

"That's blasphemy," said Mrs. Middleton.

"That's a genuine prayer," said the butler, a smile lighting up his clever comedian's face. Angus MacGregor was peeling potatoes. Rainbird leaned over, extracted six, and proceeded to juggle them expertly. "Keeping my hand in," he said. "I may go back to working the fairgrounds like I did as a boy."

"Don't even say such a thing," said Mrs. Middleton. The "Mrs." was a courtesy title, and the spinster harboured hopes of being able to marry the butler once they had their pub.

When Mrs. Middleton saw that pub in her mind's eye, it was always summer, a sparkling English summer filled with the scent of roses and honeysuckle, and lazy with the drone of bees. It would be a fairly new building, not one of those dreadful Tudor places. The Tudors never could build anything right with their low beams that hit you on the head, and their nasty thatched roofs which harboured rats, and their non-existent drains, mused Mrs. Middleton, who was convinced the Tudors had built like that out of sheer wilful spite rather than ignorance. She would never wear black again, but ginghams and colored lawns and muslins. She would rarely wear an apron, so that the customers would know she was the lady of the house and that the landlord was her husband. Rainbird would change, become stately and distinguished, and cease to remember his juggling or his acrobatics or magic tricks. Perhaps if they were really successful, they could expand into a posting house, and have droves of servants to attend to all the lords and ladies who came to stay. In her imagination, Mrs. Middleton could see the portly bulk of the Prince of Wales descending from his carriage outside the posting house as she and Rainbird stood on the steps to greet him. And then just as she was curtsying to His Royal Highness, she was jerked back to the real world by the heavily accented Scotch voice of the cook.

"I wonder if I shouldnae jist plan on goin' to Scotland," said Angus MacGregor. "I don't think I'm suited tae an English public house, and that's a fact."

"Oh, but you *are!*" cried Mrs. Middleton. Angus was a superb cook, and his cooking alone would draw the customers in droves.

"Aye, but it would take verra little to give me a wee bit o' land in Scotland and a few cattle. I would be in ma ain country and no' be at the beck and call o' anybody, ever again."

"Garn," said Dave. "Wiff a name like MacGregor, they wouldn't let you near a bit o' land. Cattle thieves, that's what the MacGregors are."

Angus was too amazed to be insulted. "Where did ye learn that?" he exclaimed.

"Lizzie gave me a book all about it," said Dave.

"Lot o' lies," muttered Angus, but he cast a sideways look at Lizzie, who was now as lost in dreams as the housekeeper had been. He had watched Lizzie change from a grubby illiterate waif to a well-read pretty young miss. But she was still a scullery maid, and surely she must begin to find her status in life increasingly degrading.

But Lizzie, too, was dreaming of the future. She would be married to Joseph, a Joseph who no longer postured and posed, but a manly Joseph, healthy and bronzed after a day's work in the fields. For Lizzie saw the pub only as an extension of her servant labours. She feared she would be a part-owner of the establishment only in name, but would be expected to scrub and clean and wait table, and never experience the joys of social status or independence. If only Joseph would consider the life of a small farmer. All they needed was a little cottage and a little piece of land. Her dreams were very much like those of the cook, but where he saw towering mountains and glittering lochs and the shaggy moorlands of Scotland, Lizzie saw the rolling English countryside where the sun always shone and where the wheat was always ripe, where the roses hung heavy over the hedge, where the grass in the garden was trim and green, a garden where she could stand in the evenings and watch Joseph striding homewards down the road.

Jenny, quick and dark, had fallen silent as well. She saw the pub only as a means to give her a background to marriage. In her dreams, she and Alice would be serving in the tap when two handsome dragoons walked in. They would be immediately smitten with both of them. Alice and she would have a double wedding. They would go to the Peninsular Wars with their husbands and be so very brave that the Prince of Wales would come to hear of it and would give them medals.

Unaware of her friend's plans for her, beautiful blond Alice dreamt of children, lots and lots of children. She adored children, and when she tried to conjure up the face of the husband who was going to give them to her, she could never quite manage it. But this nameless and faceless man would ride up to the pub one day and would take her away to a country house with large airy rooms and a large nursery.

Like Lizzie, little Dave often saw the pub as just an extension of his duties in Clarges Street. They would need someone to clean the pots, and Dave was sure that someone would always be he. The ones he loathed were the saucepans after Angus had conjured up some of his French creations. The stuff left in the bottom seemed to be made of glue. But, now, if Mr. Rainbird were to take off and go back to his life at the fairs, then Dave would go with him. They would have an easy life on the road, sleeping out under the stars, and he, Dave, would take the hat round as the crowd gasped and applauded Mr. Rainbird's clever tricks. The fairground was always brightly coloured and sunny and hot, and all the nights blazed with stars.

And then Joseph burst into the servants' hall and all the dreams of summer and the golden future whirled about their heads and disappeared.

"It's Palmer," he gasped. "Arrived in a po' chaise wiff a lady and gent. Come to see the house."

He tore off his apron and struggled into his black velvet coat. His hair was only powdered in patches and so he dusted it liberally from the flour bin until flour covered his black velvet livery like dandruff.

"It may be them!" cried Rainbird. "Our new tenants!"

He threw off his green baize apron, seized his coat from a peg at the door, and darted for the stairs.

# Chapter Two

*For the first three hours I was told it was a moonlight night, then it became cloudy, and at half past three o'clock was a rainy morning; so that I was well acquainted with every variation of the atmosphere as if I had been looking from the window all night long. A strange custom this, to pay men for telling them what the weather is every hour during the night, till they get so accustomed to the noise, that they sleep on and cannot hear what is said.*

—Robert Southey

"This 'ere's the butler," said Palmer as Rainbird darted into the hall.

The agent was standing with his stocky gaitered legs wide apart and his fat hands clasped behind his back. Beside him stood a lady and gentleman. The gentleman was tall and thin with hair so fine and so beautifully white, it looked like a spun-glass wig. His face was very odd, the nose pointing a little to the right, and the thin mouth screwed round in the same direction. He looked as if his face were desperately trying to turn a corner while the eyes remained firm, looking straight ahead. His clothes were sober and old-fashioned but of the finest material. He had a slight stoop and an oddly deferential air. Rainbird judged him to be in his fifties.

Rainbird turned his clever bright eyes on the lady and then found he could not look away. Beauty is a powerful magnet. She had clear grey-blue eyes fringed with sooty lashes. Her skin was very white and translucent. Under her small fashionable bonnet, her curls were glossy and dark brown, highlighted with little threads of gold. Her mouth was pink and warm and generous. Her eyebrows were delicate and arched, like the brush strokes of a master. She had a straight nose, a graceful neck above a ruff of fine lace, and a figure to make a sensualist swoon. But the expression in her eyes was hard and haughty.

"Stop gawking, Rainbird," snapped Palmer. "Show us around. No need to wait for that fussy Middleton female. If Mr. and Miss Goodenough like the place, then you can line up the servants."

Rainbird led the way. In the front parlour,

18

he darted about, seizing holland covers off the chairs, hoping to dispel that chill, unused atmosphere that had so repelled the Earl of Fleetwood. The fireplace was fine and Rainbird hoped they noticed it. It was marble-fronted and surmounted with a looking glass that was divided into three by gilt pillars which, in their turn, supported a gilt architrave. On either side of the fireplace were the new bell-ropes, made from coloured worsted during the winter months by Mrs. Middleton and finished by Angus, the cook, with knobs of polished spar.

The chairs and tables were of that fashionable wood, mahogany, brought from Honduras. There was a bookcase on top of a chest of drawers with glazed doors and curtains of green silk within, which could be drawn closed to shield the unintellectual eye from the dreadful sight of naked literature.

As he revealed all these wonders, Rainbird puzzled over his own odd feeling of familiarity, of recognition. He was sure he had seen this Mr. Goodenough before. That strange sideways face of his should be hard to forget. The couple said nothing as they were led from room to room, and Rainbird's heart began to sink. If only Palmer could have warned him, then he would have suggested delaying the visit to the afternoon so that the rooms might be heated and decorated with flowers.

He kept glancing at their faces, hoping to catch some hint of either approval or disapproval. But Mr. Goodenough's eyes were blank and his thin mouth was screwed up sideways in a perpetual smile. In any case, the young lady with him—his daughter? had an air of frozen hauteur that gave nothing away.

At last the tour was over and they stood in the hall, Palmer, the lady and gentleman, and Rainbird.

"We shall take it," said the young lady. Her voice was clear and accentless and very cold. "You, I know, are Rainbird, the butler. I am Miss Goodenough, and this is my uncle, Mr. Benjamin Goodenough. We shall reside here until the end of the Season on June fourth. Now, we should like to inspect the rest of the staff."

Rainbird opened the backstairs door to call the rest, but they were already crowded, waiting, on the other side of the door. He ushered them in.

Mr. Goodenough had wandered back into the front parlour and was staring vacantly out into the street. The staff shuffled into line in front of Miss Goodenough.

Her hard eye travelled down the line as Rainbird made the introductions. It came to rest on Joseph. "Brush your livery properly before you appear in front of me again," said Miss Goodenough. The footman blushed and twisted his head round, noticing the flour on his coat for the first time. Then Miss Goodenough turned her attention to Mrs. Middleton. "I shall see you this afternoon at three o'clock, Mrs. Middleton," she said. "Bring the housekeeping books with you and we shall go over them together. Thank you. That will be all."

"When," said Palmer, "will you be moving in?"

"Today," said Miss Goodenough. "Come, Uncle Benjamin," she called.

Palmer was obviously in the throes of some inner conflict. He did not want to scare them away by demanding the rent. But, on the other hand, they had arrived out of the blue, and in a rented chaise, not a private carriage.

"There is the matter of the rent," said Palmer as the Goodenoughs were making for the door. Palmer glared fiercely at Rainbird as he said this, as if in the hope the butler might get the blame if the Goodenoughs considered his demand impertinent.

"Ah, yes," said Miss Goodenough. She opened a capacious reticule and drew out a thick wad of notes, which she riffled through. Rainbird thought there must have been at least five hundred pounds in that wad. She extracted eighty pounds in five-pound and two-pound notes.

Palmer's eyes bulged in his head. "There is a little mistake, miss," he said with an ingratiating leer. "Eighty *guineas* is the sum."

"Such a pity," said Miss Goodenough. "I never deal in guineas. Nasty, heavy things. I much prefer paper money." She put the money back in her reticule. Her cool gaze rested for what seemed ages on Palmer's beefy face.

Then she said quietly, "You advertised this house at eighty pounds in *The Morning Post*. I believe you are greedily trying to chisel more money out of me. You are not getting a half farthing more. Furthermore, I have a good mind to take you to court."

"Oh, deary me!" cried Palmer, desperately feigning surprise. "My wits must be wandering. Eighty pounds it is."

"Seventy-six now," said Miss Goodenough sweetly. "You tried to make a profit of four pounds. So you can take a loss of four pounds or I shall write to the Duke of Pelham and inform him of your chicanery."

"You cannot do this!" said Palmer.

"I can and will," said Miss Goodenough.

Palmer shuffled his feet. The advertisement had now been in the newspaper for three months. The only person other than Miss Goodenough who had shown any interest was the Earl of Fleetwood, and he had decided against renting the place. Palmer looked at Miss Goodenough's set face and was sure she *would* take him to court or write to the duke—nasty, overbearing, managing female that she was.

"Very well," he muttered. "Seventy-six it is."

Miss Goodenough once more opened her reticule, extracted the wad, peeled off the necessary sum, and paid him.

"Now, Mr. Palmer," she said, "I do not like your face or your manner. Make sure you do not set foot in this house again while we have the letting of it. Come, Uncle."

Palmer and the servants stood in silence until the Goodenoughs had left and closed the door behind them.

The agent rounded savagely on the servants. "This is all your fault," he grated. "I'll make up that four pounds out of your wages." Then he left as well.

The servants shuffled back down to their hall to answer Dave's excited questions.

"She holds the purse-strings," said Rainbird, "and that Miss Goodenough is going to be the most clutch-fisted tenant we've ever had."

"S'pose we've got to put up with them," said Jenny. "Not as if there's anyone else."

"But there might be," said Angus Mac-Gregor, "if we got rid of 'em fast."

"How can we do that?" asked Mrs. Middleton, who was already shaking in her shoes at the thought of the forthcoming interview with Miss Goodenough.

"Easily," said Rainbird thoughtfully. "It is very simple for servants to drive someone away. Palmer won't listen to them. They've paid the money, he's accepted, so they can't take him to court. Good idea, Angus. But, by George, I have seen Mr. Goodenough somewhere before. If only I could remember where."

"There's so much to do," said Alice. "If they're coming this afternoon, we'd better get the beds aired and the fires lit."

Rainbird leaned back in his chair. "Why?"

he said with a grin. "If we want rid of them, we may as well begin right now by taking it easy. They'll want tea and cakes. Whip them up something really horrible, Angus!"

At The Bull's Head in the City, Miss Emily Goodenough corded the last trunk and sat back on her heels. "Well, that's that," she said. "I think we are doing very nicely."

"I think you were a leetle too high and mighty for a young miss, my dear," said Mr. Goodenough. "Mustn't give the show away."

"But I could not let that repulsive Palmer get away with cheating me!"

"And you said 'chiselling.' Ladies never talk about people chiselling people. You must try not to use common expressions. Us impostors must always be on our guard."

"We are not really impostors," said Emily. "We changed our names by deed poll. We are now Mr. and Miss Goodenough, and you are my uncle. Forget you were the butler, Benjamin Spinks, forget I was ever that little chambermaid, Emily Jenkins. We are of the upper classes now."

"Outside," said Mr. Goodenough gloomily. "But inside I still feel like a servant."

25

"But we *are* rich," said Emily. "When old Sir Harry Jackson died and left you all his money, it was like the realisation of a dream. *You* always wanted to be a gentleman, and I always wanted to marry well."

"Have you thought, Emily, that if just one member of the ton recognizes either the former butler or the former chambermaid, we should be socially damned? That butler, Rainbird, looks familiar."

For a moment, Emily appeared very young and vulnerable and lost. In that moment, she wished they were servants again, living on dreams. Then she rallied. "Fustian," she said bravely. "I shall make my début in society, and you shall meet the Prince of Wales, which is all you ever talked about. Courage, my uncle. We shall survive."

"I shall try to be brave," said Mr. Goodenough. "Wait here and I shall fetch a servant to carry our trunks. The bell-wire is broken."

When her "uncle" had left, Emily rose to her feet and studied her face in the greenish old looking-glass over the fireplace. Surely she looked like a lady!

But when she had been a servant, she had

felt like a lady inside. Now she felt like a servant inside. Odd.

Emily had been brought up by a spinster aunt. Her parents had died when she was very young. Her aunt had been a hard, unfeeling woman but prided herself on "knowing her duty." Before her death, she had secured Emily the post of chambermaid at Blackstone Hall, home of Sir Harry Jackson, a childless bachelor of some sixty years. The butler, Spinks, now Mr. Goodenough, had taken her under his wing. Like Emily, he was a dreamer, and they would often walk in the grounds at the end of the day, planning fantastic futures for each other. Emily's was always the same. Some rich lady would befriend her, bring her out as a débutante, and a rich lord would fall in love with her and marry her. The butler's dreams were wilder and more fanciful. On some evenings as he walked with Emily, he would fantasise about being a pirate king or becoming a missionary or enlisting in the army, although the one dream he would return to over and over again was that of meeting the Prince of Wales, now Prince Regent.

And while they walked and dreamt, neither guessed that old Sir Harry was shortly to die and leave all his fortune to his butler.

27

Now that they were rich, now that they were on the threshold of that long-dreamt-of Season, Emily felt the stronger of the two. Mr. Goodenough was basically a timid man. Emily often suspected he missed his days of butling. When she was married and had a title, he could live with her always, decided Emily. The years would pass and he would become accustomed to being a gentleman and no longer dread exposure.

"Pity we paid our shot in advance," said Mr. Goodenough as he came back into the room. "But I did not expect to find anywhere so quickly."

"That house has been advertised for the past three months," said Emily, "and at such a low rent. I wonder why no one else snapped it up."

"As to the matter of the rent," said Mr. Goodenough cautiously, "I feel you should have paid the full eighty pounds. Oh, I know that dreadful Palmer needed a set-down, but it was done in front of the servants, and, if you but remember, we servants have a hearty contempt for anyone who appears miserly."

Emily laughed. "I think I am forgetting more quickly than you the thoughts of a servant. Do not worry. The staff at Clarges

28

Street will have no cause to complain of my treatment."

But it was a tight-lipped Emily who stood in the front parlour at 67 Clarges Street an hour later. The fire had not been lit, and the holland covers still lay in a pile in the corner where Rainbird had thrown them that morning.

She rang the bell and waited. And waited.

After ten minutes, she gave it a savage pull.

Rainbird sauntered in and stood looking at her, eyes bright with insolence.

"You r-a-a-a-n-g?" he drawled.

"Take your hands out of your pockets when you address me," said Emily, turning pink with anger. "You will find our trunks still standing in the hall. Have them carried up to our rooms. We shall take the bedrooms on the second floor in case the large one on the first needs to be turned into a saloon. Light the fire here and light the fires everywhere else. Jump to it. And serve tea *immediately!*"

Rainbird skipped out while Emily glared furiously after him.

"My dear," quavered Mr. Goodenough, "such studied insolence does, I fear, beto-

ken that they have guessed our humble origins."

"Stuff!" said Emily roundly.

They waited impatiently as oh-so-slowly
Joseph lounged in and made up the fire,
placing lumps of coal delicately in the hearth
with the tongs, one piece at a time.

Rainbird came in with the tea-tray and
set it down on a console table with a loud
crash that made the silver clatter against the
china.

But Emily brightened. For the array of
cakes looked absolutely delicious. Her stom-
ach gave an unmaidenly rumble.

Rainbird began to skip off.

"Stop!" cried Emily. "Cannot you leave a
room in a civilised manner?"

Rainbird turned hurt eyes on her. "You
told me to jump to it, ma'am," he said
plaintively, "so I am jumping."

"When I have finished tea," said Emily
evenly, "I want you and the rest of the staff
to assemble here. Such impertinence must
cease immediately."

"Impertinence?" demanded Rainbird, folding his arms and leaning against the door-
jamb. "I—"

He broke off as a resounding volley of
knocks sounded on the street door.

He sprang to answer it.

The Earl of Fleetwood stood on the doorstep.

"I am come for another look at this place," he said, strolling in past Rainbird.

"The house is taken," cried Rainbird, but Lord Fleetwood had already entered the front parlour.

He stopped short before the vision that was Emily.

Emily looked at him, her eyes wandering from his handsome, clever face to his elegant dress, the large jewel sparkling in his cravat, and then down to those boots which had caused even Beau Brummell to turn green with envy.

"My apologies, ma'am," said the earl. "Am I to understand the house is let?"

"Yes," said Emily breathlessly. "To me."

"Me being?"

"Introduce yourself first," snapped Emily, who was quite overset by the insolence of the servants.

He raised thin brows and looked at her haughtily. "My name is Fleetwood."

"Earl of," prompted Mr. Goodenough *sotto voce*.

"Well, Lord Fleetwood, I am Miss Emily

31

Goodenough, and this is my uncle, Mr. Benjamin Goodenough."

"Your servant, Miss Goodenough. When did you decide to take the house?"

"Today, my lord."

"And you are satisfied with it?"

"Not quite," said Emily with a baleful look at Rainbird, who was staring at the cakes in a most peculiar way. "I find the staff lacking in respect. Pray be seated, my lord."

Lord Fleetwood sat down. "I confess I do not like the servant class, Miss Goodenough," he said. "I find them all prone to gossip and insolence."

Rainbird picked up the plate of cakes and headed for the door.

"Put those cakes back down immediately," said Emily crossly. "And go away, Rainbird. I shall speak to you later."

Rainbird slowly put the cakes back on the tray as Emily drew a chair up to the table and asked Lord Fleetwood if he took sugar and milk.

The butler ran downstairs to the kitchen. "Angus," he wailed, "that Lord Fleetwood has called and she is about to offer him those cakes. What did you put in them?"

"Enough curry powder to blow his head off," said the cook.

"We must stop him eating them," screamed Mrs. Middleton.

"Why?" demanded the cook laconically. "I don't like him either."

"Fleetwood is a leader of the ton, you lummox!" howled Rainbird. "This house is damned as unlucky, and now added to that will be the tale that the servants try to poison their masters. I must think of something."

Upstairs, Emily held out the plate of cakes to the earl. "Thank you, Miss Goodenough," he said, "but they look so delicious, I feel you should have first choice."

But Emily's appetite had left her. Mr. Goodenough had muttered something about seeing to his unpacking and had left the room, leaving her alone with this terrifying aristocrat. She knew, as she watched a look of surprise cross the earl's face, that it was bad ton to leave a young girl alone and unchaperoned with a gentleman.

"No, I thank you," she said. "Perhaps later."

The earl selected a large confection that appeared to be made of chocolate and cream and raised it to his mouth.

Then there came a loud shout from outside. He jumped to his feet. Outside the window, his horses were rearing and plunging while his little tiger clung desperately to the reins.

He ran from the room. Emily went to the window and was able to admire how efficiently the earl soothed down his frightened horses.

She turned about to return to her seat and let out a terrified scream as a large grey rat scuttled into the room, followed by The Moocher, the kitchen cat. She jumped up on her chair, holding up her skirts. Rainbird ran in after the cat, crashed into the table, and sent the tea service and cakes flying across the room. Dave erupted into the front parlour, deftly seized the rat by the tail, ran out again, with The Moocher in hot pursuit, and opened the front door and threw the rat out.

Unfortunately, the rat struck the returning earl full in the face and the kitchen cat jumped on him, howling and uttering warcries.

The earl pulled the stunned rat off his face and threw it into the middle of the street, where it landed in the kennel.

Emily was still screaming as he hurried into the parlour.

"This house is infested!" cried Emily. "We must leave. We cannot stay."

Despite all the shocks and alarms, the earl could not help noticing that her ankles revealed by her pulled-up skirts were absolutely beautiful.

"It was only a rat," he said soothingly. He helped her solicitously down from the chair. "What a set of happenings! My tiger tells me that some red-headed giant jumped up and down in front of the horses shouting, "Boo!" at the top of his voice.

"It's those poxy servants," said Emily bitterly. "Bad cess to 'em."

From the sudden chill in the earl's eyes, Emily realised miserably that her newly acquired refined speech had slipped into vulgarity.

She tried to compose herself. She said she would ring for more tea. But the earl's face had become a polite social blank. He sent his regards to her uncle, he was sad the house had been let, but assured her with patently false gallantry that it could not have been let to a more charming tenant, and bowed his way out.

Emily ran upstairs to pour out her troubles to Mr. Goodenough, only to find he was fast asleep in a chair in the bedroom.

She trailed back down to the front parlour. She would have to tackle these terrible servants herself.

Emily was twenty years of age, and her recently adopted haughty manner often made her look older, but as she threw herself down in a chair beside the fire and burst into tears, she looked little more than a child.

Joseph opened the door of the parlour, a dustpan and brush in his hand ready to sweep up the mess, saw the weeping Emily, and backed out in confusion, bumping into Rainbird. He whispered to the butler that Miss was in distress and they were joined by Mrs. Middleton, who was twitching like a nervous rabbit and clutching the housekeeping books to her chest. Together they peered round the door of the parlour at the miserably sobbing Emily, and then quietly closed the door and stood together in the hall.

"Poor child," whispered Mrs. Middleton.

"It goes to my heart to see her like that," muttered Rainbird. "I shall give her a few moments to compose herself and then I shall go in there and apologise."

Emily at last dried her eyes and was reaching for the bell-rope to summon Rainbird when the contrite butler appeared before her. He apologised for all the mishaps and for his own behaviour, and although he offered no explanation, Emily was relieved and at the same time touched.

As Rainbird apologised, Jenny and Joseph cleaned up the mess, Alice carried in bowls of flowers, bought earlier in case a new tenant should arrive after the rout of the Goodenoughs, Joseph made up the fire, and Angus himself appeared with tea and biscuits.

Emily rallied wonderfully under all this attentive kindness.

By the time Mrs. Middleton came in with the books, Emily found she was beginning to enjoy herself discussing household matters. She asked how much they all earned and exclaimed in surprise over the small amount. Rainbird, without much hope, for he still feared Miss Goodenough would prove tight-fisted, murmured that previous tenants had seen fit to augment their wages for the length of the Season, and to his surprise, Emily readily agreed to this.

The household budget she proposed was extremely generous.

Emily tried to maintain an aloof manner with these odd servants, frightened that they might become too familiar again should she be over-friendly, but soon found herself chatting easily with Mrs. Middleton and Rainbird about plans to send cards out for a rout so as to lay the ground for her forthcoming début.

Mr. Goodenough did not wake until dinner time, unaware of all the battles that had been fought and won while he slept. He was delighted to hear how friendly, helpful, and efficient the servants had proved to be and, mellowed by good food and excellent wine, began to look more confident than he had done since he had gained his inheritance. Emily somehow could not bring herself to tell him about the end to the Earl of Fleetwood's disastrous visit. She knew he would be alarmed and frightened when he learned of her slip into common language. It was wonderful to see this, her patron, looking happy and at ease, for he was facing up to the rigours of a London Season solely for her sake.

Downstairs, the servants settled down late in the evening to their supper, just as relaxed and happy as Mr. Goodenough.

"A pleasant, quiet, genteel couple," said

Mrs. Middleton. "Oh, Mr. Rainbird, it appears as if we shall have our first *comfortable* Season."

"Amen to that!" said Rainbird, raising his glass. "What a monstrous rat, Angus. How did you find it so quickly?"

"Got it frae the rat-catcher earlier," said the cook. "I originally planned tae put it in Miss Goodenough's bed. Well, it's just as well I did not, for she has turned out to be a good lady. I hope that Lord Fleetwood never finds out it was me that startled his horses."

It was to be Emily's first night in London. She had never slept anywhere other than in the country before. Every time she was on the point of dropping off to sleep, the watchman would come along the street below, shouting it was a fine moonlit night and all was well. He came along with his weather bulletin every half hour. Added to that were the cries and rumbles of the night coaches going along Piccadilly at the end of Clarges Street. No sooner had their din ceased, than the clatter of the morning carts began. Then came the dustman with his bell, bellowing, "Dust *ho!*" at the top of his voice, then came the watchman again. He was succeeded by the porterhouse boy, jangling and clashing his tray of pewter pots. After him came the milkman and then more and more numerous cries, a deafening cacophony, but pierced always, every half-hour, by the irritating, penetrating drone of the watch.

Emily climbed down from her high bed and pulled a wrapper about her shoulders. She took a crown from her reticule and made her way downstairs. She would *pay* that watchman to go away. If he at least was silenced, then perhaps she could get some sleep.

The Earl of Fleetwood was walking back to Limmer's Hotel from his club in St. James's. He found himself in Clarges Street and wondered idly how the strange Miss Goodenough was faring with her even stranger servants.

And then he saw her.

A shaft of morning sunlight was striking the doorway of 67 Clarges Street. Between the two chained iron dogs that ornamented the front step stood Miss Emily Goodenough. She was saying something to the watchman and handing him a crown. The watch touched his hat and walked away.

Emily stood for a moment on the step, her face lifted up to the sunshine.

The sunlight lit up the gold threads in

the masses of her hair, which tumbled down her back. In her white muslin wrapper and white nightgown she looked like some princess in a fairy-tale.

There was a purity about her, and a vulnerable innocence. She was as fresh as the morning.

Strangely touched, the earl stood watching her until she turned about and went back inside.

# Chapter Three

*Last night,* party *at Landsdowne House.
Tonight,* party *at Lady Charlotte Gre-
ville's—deplorable waste of time, and something of temper. Nothing imparted—nothing acquired—talking without ideas . . .
Heigho!—and in this way half London
pass what is called life.*

—Lord Althorp

Emily was just sinking into a deep sleep
when she remembered that rat. And then
she remembered the drama caused by Lord
Fleetwood's startled horses. In the heat of
the moment, she had been sure it was all
the fault of the servants. But Rainbird had
been so apologetic . . . and yet . . . and yet,
he had not explained anything.

She tossed and turned, determined to put
the matter out of her head, but now every
creak and rustle sounded like the furtive
movements of rats.

She rang the bell.

Alice answered it, looking her usual relaxed and beautiful self.

"I shall fetch your morning chocolate directly, miss," said Alice, crossing the room to open the curtains.

"No," said Emily. "I still want to sleep, but I am troubled about that rat. Is this house *full* of rats?"

Alice, like Rainbird, had no conscience about lying when she considered it necessary. "Oh, no," she said in her slow, rich country voice. "Lord Charteris next door had the rat-catcher in and one of the rats got away. But we have no trouble on account of The Moocher, the kitchen cat. Fearsome hunter, he is."

"But why were Lord Fleetwood's horses frightened?"

"I don't know, miss. Reckon there are many odd people about London. Mr. Rainbird said a horrible-looking man shouted at them and frightened them. Will there be anything else?"

"Yes. Rainbird apologised for his earlier insolence but did not explain *why* he had been insolent. Can you tell me?"

Alice looked at Emily with wide blue eyes while she tried to think of an excuse. Then it hit her that perhaps the truth was the best explanation.

"You see, miss," said Alice, "we have mortal-poor wages, and we rely on a tenant to increase those wages. Seeing as how you was so nice over the matter of the rent, we reckoned as how you might be overnice in the matter of household expenses. And there was still time to find another tenant."

"Do you mean," said Emily wrathfully, "that you were trying to *drive* me away?"

"Sounds a bit harsh put like that," said Alice, "but times is hard. We are all ever so sorry now.'

Emily tried to stay angry, but anger was quickly being replaced by relief. They had not thought her common or despised her for her low origins. They did not know! They had merely considered her to be stingy.

"Oh," said Emily. "Well, behave your-selves in future. Perhaps I understand now why that normally deft and agile butler contrived to fall over the table. What *was* in those cakes?"

But Alice felt she had revealed enough. "Mr. MacGregor, the cook, is a genius," said Alice. "Pity them cakes was spoiled."

"It is a *pity* that Lord Fleetwood was given a disgust of this house," said Emily, although she knew it was she herself who had disaffected him. "Is he a great personage?"

"Yes, miss. Mr. Rainbird do say as how Lord Fleetwood is a leader of society. This is his second Season in London since the death of his wife, although she died eight years ago.

"And how did she die?" Emily felt she was being very vulgar gossiping with a servant, but her curiosity about the handsome earl was becoming stronger by the minute.

"She was beaten to death in a wood near his country home, miss."

"Gracious! Who was responsible?"

"Nobody ever found out, miss," said Alice, who, like Jenny, had no time for Luke's gossip and did not believe a word of the next-door footman's story of Lord Fleetwood's having committed the murder himself.

Emily felt she should now dismiss Alice, but she had not conversed with any member of her own sex for such a long time. "You are very pretty, Alice," said Emily. "Did that not cause you some trouble with the previous gentleman tenants of this house?" Emily suddenly remembered some of her own experiences as a chambermaid while Sir Harry Jackson had still been well enough to entertain.

"No, miss. Mr. Rainbird would never allow such a thing. One gentleman," said Alice, remembering the arrival of last year's handsome tenant, "got a bit frisky at first, but after Mr. Rainbird spoke to him I didn't have no trouble."

"Thank you, Alice," said Emily, who felt she had been indulging in gossip for long enough. "You may go."

Alice went out quietly and closed the door.

Emily snuggled down under the blankets. So the servants had not seen under her mask after all! No one would, she reassured herself fiercely. Sir Harry's estates had been in Cumberland, in the far north of England. Such guests as he had entertained had usually come from the local county, and only one or two travellers had stopped over on their road to London.

A shadow fell across Emily's face. It was one of those travellers who had tried to force his attentions on her, a horrible man —Mr. Percival Pardon. Her screams had brought Mr. Goodenough, then the butler, Spinks, running to her aid. The row that had ensued had caused the poor butler to have an apoplexy from which he had recovered but which had left his face peculiarly twisted up. Shortly after that unfortunate visit, Sir Harry had fallen ill and entertained no more.

Surely no one in London would recognise the chambermaid Emily Jenkins in the now rich and fashionable Emily Goodenough, or the butler Spinks in the changed face of the now Benjamin Goodenough, Esquire.

They had laid their plans well. They had not dashed off to London, but had gone about things slowly and carefully. The house and estates had been sold, and then they had travelled south to Bath, so that Emily might study the manners of the ladies, and have a fashionable wardrobe made. They had spent a whole year in Bath becoming accustomed to their new identities, although they took no part in the society of the spa.

Somewhere in London, thought Emily, as her eyes began to close, must be a gentleman of manners and title who would want her for a wife. Lord Fleetwood would not do at all, even if it turned out she had not given him a dislike of her, thought Emily, banishing the earl's handsome face from her mind. Any man who despised servants as much as he must be cold and unfeeling.

"Why do you persist in staying in this disgusting hotel?" demanded the Earl of Fleetwood's sister, Mrs. Mary Otterley. "You have a perfectly good town house in Grosvenor Square."

"Which you are living in at the moment," pointed out the earl. "I did not expect you to take it for this Season as well."

"I do not see what the trouble is," said Mrs. Otterley crossly. "You were quite content to stay with us last year."

"If I may remind you of last year," said the earl gently, "I came to the Season to find myself a wife. No sooner had I found a likely candidate than you saw fit to call on the girl and her parents, and after that I found I was not welcome."

"Nothing to do with me," said Mrs. Otterley. She was a fat, square, pugnacious, red-faced woman, some ten years older than the earl.

"And yet, I was under the impression, Mary, that it was you who reminded my lady-love of the peculiar nature of my late wife's death."

"Stuff! Would I do such a thing?"

"Your son, Clarence, stands to inherit my title and estates if I do not wed and have children of my own. I am warning you, Mary, do not interfere again."

Mrs. Otterley buried her dry eyes in a handkerchief and gave a very stage-like sob. "That my own brother should accuse me of such a thing! Poor Clarissa. How can you forget her so soon?"

"Easily," said the earl brutally. "Clarissa, my lovely wife, has been dead these past eight years."

"I cannot understand what went wrong with that marriage," said his sister, giving up pretending to cry. "Clarissa was so beautiful, so dainty, so much a lady . . ."

"And childless," said the earl, "so naturally you approved of her. I did not talk to you about my marriage at the time, Mary, and I have no intention of talking about it now. I had enough of a cross to bear with those Sussex servants at Whitecross Hall. They tattled and gossiped so much, it was a wonder I was not hanged outside Newgate. I detest malicious gossips, and my detestation of all servants makes me reluctant to set about finding a place in London. The servants I have now in Sussex are hand-picked and as close-mouthed as clams. They are all good country people, unlike the last lot, who were mostly imports from London."

"No girl will marry you," said Mrs. Otterley. "You are too hard and unfeeling."

"Any woman will marry me for my title and fortune, provided you do not turn up on her doorstep with tales of murder. I do not look for love, simply for good breeding and refined manners."

"All I have to say is," began his sister, but then she broke off as an elegant exquisite was ushered into the earl's suite of rooms. "Oh, here's that poisonous fribble. I'm off."

As the door slammed behind her, the earl turned to the new arrival with a sweet smile and said, "Sit down, Fitz. You are a sight for sore eyes. Nothing endears me more to you than your ability to rout my Friday-faced sister."

Mr. Jason Fitzgerald dropped languidly into an armchair opposite the earl. He was a tall, thin man and, like the earl, in his early thirties. He had very fair hair, which was teased and backcombed up on top of his head. His collars were judged to be the highest in London and so ferociously starched that the points left little red marks on his cheekbones. Despite his thin body, he had a pair of long, well-shaped muscular legs which were that morning encased in skin-tight pantaloons of bright yellow. His face was highly painted. He had a noble forehead and a proud nose, but his receding chin was his private despair and he disguised it by having an intricately tied cravat rising up in front to shield it. A shrapnel wound in his back had put an end to his army career and often made walking and dancing an agony, but he covered up his pain with his usual mask which was that of a frivolous dandy, and only the earl knew how much of a mask it was and how Fitz longed to be fit enough to re-enlist.

"I have found a house for you," said Fitz languidly. "Take you there now, if you like. Pretty place. No servants. Hire your own."

"Where is it?"

"Park Lane."

"Nobody admits to living in Park Lane!"

"You are behind the times. They do now. Come. I'll show you."

Park Lane, the erstwhile Tyburn Lane of dubious repute, though still unevenly paved and patched with leftover material from building sites, had rapidly improved its social standing with the disappearance of the mobs who used to make their way along it to the gallows to watch the public hangings.

Now the public hangings were performed outside Newgate Prison in the City. Until a very short time ago, the residents of Park Lane had kept a high wall between themselves and the street, having their mansions fronting onto Park Street, and their gardens running down to that high wall which hid the view, not only of Park Lane, but of Hyde Park itself.

But the house Fitz had picked out for his friend belonged to a Mr. Warwick Wyman, an architect, who had received permission from the government's Department of Woods and Forests to take down the section of wall at the end of his garden. He had then set about turning the back of the house into the front, building pleasant bay windows and delicate wrought-iron balconies and verandahs and a graceful colonnaded entrance.

Mr. Wyman turned out to be there in person to show them around.

Thanks to his improvements, the house proved to be one of the most well-lit and airy in London. Red Turkey carpet was fitted throughout with fleecy hearthrugs—a new invention—before each marble fireplace. Also new were the fire-guards, huge affairs of brass netting supported by brass pillars. Mr. Wyman told them he delighted in new inventions and showed them his collection. There was a razor for shaving yourself while galloping on horseback, a pocket toasting-fork, a machine for slicing cucumbers, a Patent Compound Concave Corkscrew, stamped *Ne plus ultra* by the inventor to warn all future would-be corkscrew makers that the art of making corkscrews could be carried no further, and Mr. Wyman's pride and joy—a portable fender complete with portable pocket-sized fire-irons.

The Earl of Fleetwood politely complimented Mr. Wyman on this last treasure, carefully hiding his sudden doubt about the sanity of this architect. For who but a madman would travel with his own fender and fire-irons? And what did Mr. Wyman do in inn or country house with the existing fender and fire-irons in his room? Throw them out of the window? Or did he plan to visit some aboriginal country where the inhabitants did not have fenders?

But the character of Mr. Wyman, as they moved from room to room, emerged as that of a pleasant and clever eccentric, rather than that of a madman.

The rooms were all well-appointed. In the main drawing room, the curtains were of rich printed cotton, lined with a plain colour and fringed with silk. Above the curtains was a sconce divided into six prints in gilt frames. Two of these were of Noel's view of Cádiz and Lisbon and the others were from English history and represented the battles of the Boyne and of La Hogue, the death of General Wolfe at Quebec, and William Penn treating with the Indians for his province of Pennsylvania.

The rent for the Season was seven hundred and fifty pounds. The earl thought ruefully of that house in Clarges Street, which he could have had for a mere eighty, but he had fallen in love with the Park Lane mansion and it was at least four times the size of that other house. After only a little token haggling, he agreed to meet Mr. Wyman's price.

"I could but wish," said the earl, "that among your inventions were a set of mechanical servants. I have no love of the breed."

"Alas," said Mr. Wyman, "I am afraid your lordship must rely on the human article. I can recommend a good agency."

"No," said the earl. "I shall fetch my own servants from the country. I have recently engaged new staff who can be guaranteed not to tattle or gossip."

After sharing a bottle of port with Mr. Wyman, the earl and Fitz set out to walk across Hyde Park and amble round the Serpentine.

"I shall be glad to move out of that hotel," sighed the earl. "It is excessively expensive and excessively dirty. I hope this Season proves to be less boring than the last. What an empty, shallow life we lead in Town. Empty conversations spiced with even emptier flirtations. Still, I have already had one adventure. Did I tell you I went to see that damned and accursed house in Clarges Street?"

"No. Did the ghosts come out of the wainscoting and jangle their chains at you?"

"I went twice, and no, it was not haunted. The second time I went—for I had refused it on the first visit and then thought I might perhaps take it after all—I found it already tenanted, and by quite the most beautiful female I ever beheld."

"She does not exist! She was some fairy!"

"Not she. And in moments of stress, of the earth, earthy."

"Who is this paragon?"

"A Miss Emily Goodenough."

"Ah, she will turn out to be your chambermaid, Emilia."

"Shhh. Can you imagine how damned I would be if anyone but you knew I wrote books? Did you like it? The latest one, I mean. It is to be published soon."

"It was flattering to be allowed to read it before the publisher, and I enjoyed it very much. I recognised many members of the ton in it. You have a keen eye and a biting wit, my friend. But I did not recognise Emilia. Poor girl. You certainly vented all your dislike of servants on her. It was a bit far-fetched, too. No chambermaid, however beautiful, could foist herself on the London ton."

"It's fiction," laughed the earl. "Only fiction."

"Then let us return to fact. The beautiful Miss Goodenough. What caused the stress?"

"While we were conversing, and I quite smitten with her beauty, two things happened. My horses outside took fright, and I returned in time to find Miss Goodenough standing on a chair—revealing, I may say, ankles to make a strong man faint—and screaming her head off while a sort of House That Jack Built situation raged around her. A rat was being chased by a cat which was being chased by a small boy who was being chased by a butler who knocked over the tea-table. But I exaggerate. That was what appeared to have happened. I was not on the scene at the time, but as I returned after quietening my horses, I received the rat full in the face and the claws of the kitchen cat as it jumped up me to get at the rat.

"The beautiful divinity blamed the servants. She appeared to think they had contrived all."

"And had they?"

"I do not think any London servants would dare to go so far."

"And was that when Miss Goodenough fell from her pedestal?"

"Yes. She blamed the servants in language that was common to say the least."

"Just like your Emilia!" cried Fritz. "*That* is when her swain sees the dross beneath the gold. You were hard on her, I must say. You might have let her marry her lord."

The earl laughed. "And be a model for other presumptuous chambermaids? Never!"

"I confess I have a burning desire to see Miss Goodenough. Has she parents?"

"No. An odd sort of uncle with a twisted face."

"And a sinister sneer?"

"Who is the novelist? You or I? No, a gentleman of apologetic and deferential mien. He departed before all the drama, leaving me alone with Miss Emily."

"Very unconventional. And so Miss Emily has feet of clay. She lies in ruins at the bottom of her pedestal."

"Well . . ." said the earl reluctantly, "I happened to be walking along Clarges Street early the morning after and she was paying the watchman—to go away, I think—and she stood on the step in the sunlight with her hair down her back in only her nightgown and wrapper."

"Worse and worse and commoner and commoner. You gave a shudder and kept on walking."

"On the contrary," said the earl, "I stood there gazing on all that freshness and innocence and beauty and thought I had never seen anything quite so exquisite or quite so touching in my life before."

"Odso! You are become romantic at last, my friend. No more shall we have to smart under the lash of your tongue in those bitter novels of yours!"

"Not I," said the earl. "I shall avoid Miss Emily in the future for fear she may open her mouth and ruin quite the most beautiful picture I ever beheld!"

Lizzie, the scullery maid, hurried back to 67 Clarges Street from Shepherd Market. She had been sent out to buy black pepper for Angus, the cook, and although the market was just around the corner, she had spent more time there than was necessary, enjoying the unexpected warmth of the weak early spring sunlight.

She had changed in appearance from the small, frail child who had taken up employ some years before. Her hair, regularly washed despite warnings from the other servants that it was a dangerous habit liable to cause all sorts of inflammations and "dampness in the brain," was thick and glossy and of a rich brown. It was confined at the nape of her neck with a cherry-red silk ribbon, a present from a previous tenant. Her new cotton gown, made by herself under Mrs. Middleton's instruction that winter, was white with a thin green stripe. It was of coarse cotton and unlike the fine India muslins worn by the ladies, but it looked fresh and neat.

She was not looking where she was going as she turned into Clarges Street, being lost in her favourite day-dream of marriage to Joseph, and she nearly collided with Luke, the Charterises' first footman. Lizzie murmured an apology, stepped backwards, and dropped Luke a curtsy, a first footman being high above a scullery maid in the servants' pecking order.

"Look where you're going next time," said Luke ungraciously. He was as tall as Joseph and wore his black hair powdered. He was wearing new livery, red plush laced with gold.

"Yes, Mr. Luke," said Lizzie meekly, anxious to get away, for she did not like Luke and thought he was a bad influence on Joseph.

As she turned away, Luke noticed the wealth of Lizzie's shining hair and the trimness of her figure.

"Wait a bit, Lizzie," he said. "You are looking very fine these days. Quite the little lady."

"Thank you," whispered Lizzie, avoiding his bold gaze.

"P'raps you'd care to step out with me of an evening," said Luke.

Lizzie was human enough to blush with pleasure. It was a great honour for a scullery maid to be asked out by a first footman.

Although she had no intention of walking out with Luke, she did not want to annoy him by refusing his offer there and then.

"I would need to have Mr. Rainbird's permission," said Lizzie. "We have a new tenant and we're ever so busy."

"I'll ask old Rainbird," said Luke with a grin. "Tell him to expect me."

Lizzie bobbed another curtsy and then ran towards Number 67.

"Fetching little thing," thought Luke. "Bound to be grateful to me for the honour."

"Mr. Rainbird will tell him to go away," thought Lizzie, but she still glowed with pleasure at the compliment.

# Chapter Four

*. . . land of* punch romaine *and plate,*
*Of dinners fix'd at half-past eight;*
*Of morning lounge, of midnight rout,*
*Of debt and dun, of love and gout,*
*Of drowsy days, of brilliant nights,*
*Of dangerous eyes, of downright frights.*
                    —May Fair, Anon.

Miss Emily Goodenough had not yet grasped that to know nobody in London was to *be* a Nobody.

With the help of Mr. Goodenough, she studied the social columns in the newspapers and planned whom to invite to her first rout.

She longed to plunge into that glittering world of society she saw all about her when she went out for walks accompanied by Joseph. And when she was at home, studying the magazines and newspapers, it was maddening to hear noise and laughter from the street as people made calls and received calls and went for drives, or to stand by the window watching them setting out for balls, glittering with jewels, and know that all these members of society were as yet unaware of Miss Goodenough.

Mr. Goodenough was well-versed in all the names of the notables, having made a study of them all when he had been in service in Cumberland. That was why he had recognised the earl's name so promptly. But, like Emily, he assumed a lavish entertainment would soon bring floods of invitations pouring in. Naïvely, the ex-servants thought that to be rich was enough.

"Should we ask the Earl of Fleetwood?" asked Emily one evening.

"By all means," said Mr. Goodenough. "He is a social leader."

Emily hesitated before drawing forward one of the gilt cards with the legend "At Home"—for one spoke about inviting people to a rout, but the invitation always simply said that so-and-so would be at home on a certain evening. The earl had made her feel uncomfortable. She cursed her own slip of the tongue.

In the hope that her niece would rise in service to the level of lady's maid, Emily's aunt, Miss Cummings, had schooled Emily's voice to eradicate her soft Cumbrian burr, but had failed to correct the content of her speech. Miss Cummings had a nasty habit of becoming broad and coarse-mouthed when she had taken too much gin, and Emily had grown up innocently trotting out some of her aunt's choice phrases. Although Mr. Goodenough had done much to correct her, Emily still felt all those horrible coarse phrases were lurking around in the back of her mind, ready to leap out at the wrong moment.

Then there was surely more to learn that she had ever dreamt of in Bath. She had listened eagerly to the speech of the young London débutantes as they shopped in Oxford Street and was amazed to find that the fashionable method of speech was a babylike lisp. You became "oo," walk became "walkies," and drives "tiddle-poms in the Park." It was all very baffling. She could not hope to master this strange lingo in such a short time, but provided she kept her voice free of cant and coarse expressions, she would survive.

She thought of the earl and thought of his social position and reluctantly penned his name on the invitation. Emily did not aspire to wed an earl. A younger son of a peer, Sir

Somebody, or a plain esquire would do very well.

As the day on which the rout was to be held approached, Emily plunged into a frenzy of shopping until Joseph, who accompanied her everywhere, wailed that his feet were being "destroyed." She bought jewels, she bought feathers, gloves, fans, and silk flowers. She ordered banks of hothouse flowers to decorate the rooms and, unaware that a rout was not usually blessed with either refreshments or entertainment, hired a small orchestra.

She was rather puzzled that no one had called or replied in any way to any of her invitations, but assumed that was the way of the ton. If all these grand people were *not* coming, then they would have surely written to say so. Mr. Goodenough had tried to reassure her by saying that many things were conducted differently in the country.

The day of the rout was depressing. A soaking drizzle wept from the grey skies. Emily fought down the feeling that the weather was a bad omen. But *she* was ready for the whole of fashionable London, and the servants were behaving in a calm and unflurried manner.

It was as well Emily could not hear the frantic discussion in the servants' hall.

"I really do not think poor Miss Good-enough knows what she is doing," said Mrs. Middleton. "She says she is expecting at least a hundred people. How can we fit one hundred into this tiny house?"

"Crushes are fashionable," said Rainbird. "Society thinks a rout is a success if they have been crushed and beaten and trampled on."

"But what troubles me," said Mrs. Middleton, her nose twitching in distress, "is that I do not believe our Miss Emily *knows* anyone. No one has been to call, except that Fleetwood, and *he* only came because he thought he might take the house after all."

"That's right," said Joseph, coming in at the end of Mrs. Middleton's worries. "I've been round to The Running Footman, and Luke says—"

"Luke says. Luke *says*," jeered Jenny.

"He knows what's he's talking about," said Joseph huffily. "He has been talking to Lord Fleetwood's butler, Giles, what is just come up from the country, his lordship having taken a house in Park Lane. Giles says his master got this invitation from Miss Goodenough and he overheard Lord Fleetwood say to his friend, Mr. Fitzgerald, 'I think it wiser not to go.' *And* then Luke says as how Lord and Lady Charteris thought it *presumptuous* of Miss Goodenough to send them invitations when she don't know them or anybody else. *Then* Lord Frankland's valet says as how everyone's saying, 'Who is this mushroom?' and how Brummell said in White's t'other day, 'I shall not go. Not *good enough* for me,' which everyone thought was monstrous funny."

"But Miss Emily has spent a fortune on food and flowers and an orchestra," said Mrs. Middleton. "I wanted to tell her that all these things were not necessary for a rout, but she is rather cold and haughty, and I did not like to tell her what to to do."

"Yes, she *has* been very unapproachable and frosty," said Rainbird. "I wonder what brought that about. She did seem to have accepted my apology, but later, the day after that, she looked at me as if I had crawled in from the kennel."

"Reckon I know something about that," said Alice slowly.

"Come on, Alice," urged Jenny. "What happened?"

There was a long pause while they waited for Alice's brain to crank into action.

Then Alice said, "She was asking about the rat and the horses and all, and I told her lies about them. But then she asked me why Mr. Rainbird had been so insolent and, well, I told the truth."

*"You what!"* screamed several voices in unison.

"Couldn't think of a lie," said Alice. "Told her we thought she was being a bit cheap over the matter of the rent and that we feared she might be cheap with us, so we tried to get rid of her."

"And what did she say to that?" asked Mrs. Middleton faintly.

"Says something like, don't do it again, and looks relieved."

"How can we help the poor girl now?" said Rainbird crossly. "If we try to advise her as to how to go on, she will think we are plotting against her."

"Pity she isn't someone who *has* to keep her background a secret, like in those books I read," said Lizzie dreamily. "You know, like she's really a foreign princess in disguise."

"Worth a try," said Angus MacGregor. "Thae totty-heids in society would believe anything, provided someone told them it was a secret."

"You really mean we should go ahead with it?" asked Rainbird, amazed.

"Why not?" said Angus with a shrug. "I dinnae want to see all this food go tae waste."

"There's one other thing," said Mrs. Middleton. "Miss Emily does not seem to know that it will be considered very odd in her, should anyone at all turn up, not to be accompanied by a female companion. A young lady, hopeful of marriage, should always be launched by some female."

"Wait there!" said Rainbird. "First I must go and see if I can melt Miss Goodenough's icy manner or we will not get anywhere at all. There's the door. See who it is, Dave."

Dave came back, looking puzzled. "It's Luke," he said. "And he wants to speak to you, Mr. Rainbird."

"Not Joseph?"

"No, you."

Rainbird went to the door. After only a few moments, he returned, looking highly amused. "Well, well," he said. "Wonders will never cease. That was Luke asking permission to walk out with Lizzie."

Lizzie blushed and avoided Joseph's startled look.

"I said I'd think about it," said Rainbird, "and sent the whipper-snapper on his way.

69

Come along, Joseph. No need to sit there looking as if you've been struck by lightning. Clean the silver while I soften Miss Goodenough's flinty heart."

Emily's face set in a hard and haughty mask as Rainbird entered the room. After her relief at Alice's revelation had worn off, Emily felt that she, Emily, had not behaved in a proper manner. She should have reported the servants to Palmer and found somewhere else. But jewels and fine feathers could be sold should the Season prove to be a disaster. An enormous rent would have drained a significant amount of their capital away, and although they had a great deal of money, Emily always reminded herself it was Mr. Goodenough's money, and it was her duty to cut a dash and yet be as thrifty as possible. So she had stayed, but had tried to convey her displeasure to the servants by being as chilly and aloof as possible.

"Yes, Rainbird?" she demanded.

"Where is Mr. Goodenough?" asked Rainbird.

"He is resting in his room. Do you wish to speak to him?"

"No, ma'am, I wish to speak to you in private. I apologised to you for my previous insolence, but Alice has only just told me that she had explained the reason for my insolence. I am here to apologise again."

"I shall consider your apology," said Emily loftily. "Whether I accept it or not will depend on your future behaviour."

"But we have no time to *wait* for my future behaviour to prove my good intentions," said Rainbird. "Miss Goodenough, you are desperately in need of our help *now*."

"Why, pray?"

"Because no one is going to come to this rout this evening," said Rainbird. "They don't know who you are and they consider it impertinent of you to have even invited them."

"No one is coming?" whispered Emily, turning white. "No one?"

Rainbird shook his head.

"Then there is nothing to be done," said Emily, trying not to cry.

"But there is," said Rainbird eagerly. "First, you must leave it to us to make you fashionable. Secondly, you must have a female companion. No young lady launches *herself* on a Season."

Emily was too upset and bewildered to

keep up her haughty front. "But I don't know any gentlewomen!" she wailed.

Rainbird thought quickly and then his face cleared. "Mrs. Middleton!" he cried. "The housekeeper. She is of genteel family and knows how to go on. *She* will serve for this evening as chaperone."

"But what is the point of her serving as anything," said Emily dismally, "if no one is going to come?"

"They will! They will!" said Rainbird.

"But how? I know . . . you are going to spread gossip about me to excite their curiosity. What gossip? I must know, Rainbird."

"We are going to say you are a foreign princess who has kept herself alone for fear of being beset by adventurers and mushrooms."

"No one will believe such a thing!"

"They will," said Rainbird. "Oh yes, they will."

"But won't they want to know which country I am princess of?"

"No one will dare offend you by asking. Should anyone do so, you laugh and say you are nobody but plain Miss Goodenough. They won't believe you."

Colour slowly came back to Emily's cheeks. "If you think such a lie would work," she said cautiously. "Only my uncle must not know of it. He is not strong."

"No, miss."

"So, my wise butler, have you any suggestions as to how I should behave to give credence to this lie?"

Rainbird looked at the small stately figure, at the beautiful face and luxuriant hair. "I would say simply behave like yourself, Miss Emily. You look like a princess."

Emily began to laugh and she was still laughing when Rainbird bowed and left the room.

A princess? Why not? Emily wiped her streaming eyes. If she was going to be an impostor, she might as well do things in style!

"Are you sure you are determined not to go to Miss Goodenough's rout?" asked Fitz later that day. "I have not been invited, so I need you to take me."

"I am going to the opera instead," said the earl. He swung about. "Giles," he said to his butler. "Stop shuffling around in that furtive manner and pour Mr. Fitzgerald a drink, and then you may leave."

"Yes, my lord," said Giles. He was bursting with all the gossip he had just heard at

The Running Footman about Miss Emily Goodenough. He knew his master would not listen to any servants' gossip and furthermore would be annoyed to learn his butler had passed most of the day in a public house instead of visiting the wine merchants where he was supposed to have been.

That butler, Rainbird, had been extremely kind to Giles. Quite like an old friend the way he had confided his worries about his mistress. Giles had promised to help, but how could a butler help when he was not supposed to gossip?

He slowly poured Mr. Fitzgerald a glass of canary while he wondered how to introduce the subject.

"Are you *still* here, Giles?" came his master's voice.

"I was wondering, my lord," said Giles, "if your lordship would object to my taking the evening off."

"I don't think I shall need you this evening, Giles. Are you succumbing to the temptations of London this early in the day?"

"No, my lord. I met the butler from Number 67 Clarges Street and he asked me to call on him this evening."

"Number 67? No, you may not go. I

happen to know they are holding a rout there and their butler will have no time to entertain you. He is simply trying to get some unpaid help."

"On the contrary, my lord," said Giles, "he does not expect to be working at all. It is well known that no one is going to attend Miss Goodenough's rout."

"And why is that?"

"Because no one has ever heard of her. Perhaps if they knew she was really a foreign princess . . . but alas, they consider her a Nobody. Mr. Brummell was heard to say that Miss Goodenough was not Good Enough for him. Quite a laugh it caused in the club."

"Enough! I am not interested in the tittle-tattle of dandies. You may leave."

"And may I have the evening off?"

"Poor little Miss Goodenough," murmured Fitz. "That settles it. If no one who is invited is going, then she will be glad to see someone who is not. I shall go. Is she really a princess, do you suppose?"

"Not for a moment," said the earl. "Oh, very well, Fitz. We shall both go, but I shall not stay above ten minutes. You may have the evening off, Giles, but you are not to work, and if the Clarges Street servants are busy, then you must return here."

"Yes, my lord," said Giles.

"A good man, that," said the earl after his butler had left the room. "But he has had no previous experience of London and I don't want him led astray by London servants. At least he does not gossip."

"And how did you get on with old frosty-face?" asked the first footman, Silas, as Giles entered the servants' hall.

"I've got him to go," said Giles triumphantly. "*And* I've got the evening off meself so I can see all the fun. Managed to drop that bit about her being a princess. Tell you what, Silas, let's help that Rainbird fellow a bit further. Drop round next door to Lord Allington's servants' hall and have a bit of a gossip. . . ."

Rainbird, Joseph, and Angus worked The Running Footman, which was the upper servants' pub, in shifts, gossiping and gossiping. Like a stone dropped in a pool, the gossip spread outwards and outwards in ripples, as servants talked to servants, and servants then talked to masters and mistresses.

Mrs. Middleton was closeted with Emily,

76

being dressed to look like the companion to a foreign princess. At last she was attired in a combination of her own wardrobe and Emily's, in purple silk and purple turban and with one of Emily's new diamond necklaces about her neck, Emily not knowing that diamonds were completely exploded. Everything that was no longer in fashion was said to be "exploded."

Mrs. Middleton looked so imposing and at the same time so reassuring that Emily decided to ask her for help.

"My mother was a very great lady, Mrs. Middleton," lied Emily, "but did not give birth to me until she was in her forties. Consequently her speech was still coarse—it *was* fashionable to be coarse in Mama's youth—and I unfortunately am subject to slips. Please be on your guard to cover up for me should I forget myself."

Mrs. Middleton readily agreed. Inside, she was feeling as nervous as Emily and hoped that the gossip would not work and that no one would come.

# Chapter Five

*My dear Lady——! I've been just sending out*
*About five hundred cards for a snug little*
*rout—But I can't conceive how, in this very*
*cold weather, I'm ever to bring my five*
*hundred together . . . . . . in short, my dear,*
*names like*
  *Wintztschitstopschinzoudhoff*
  *Are the only things now to make an*
*evening smooth off—*
  *So, get me a Russian—till death I'm*
*your debtor—*
  *If he brings the whole alphabet so much*
*the better.*
  *And—Lord! if he would but in*
*character, sup*
  *Off his fish-oil and candles, he'd quite*
*set me up!*
  *Au revoir, my sweet girl—I must leave*
*you in haste—*
  *Little Gunter has brought me*
*the liquors to taste.*

—Thomas Moore

"Will she be expecting you, do you think?" asked Fitz, as he and the earl strolled along Curzon Street.

"I do not know, my friend."

"Surely you gave some reply to her invitation?"

"I never reply to invitations unless they be to dinner. I either go or don't go."

"I confess to certain tremors of excitement," said Fitz. "Is she really so beautiful?"

"Miss Goodenough is extremely beautiful and very much out of the common way."

"What is this ridiculous story about her being a princess?"

"It is a usual practice," said the earl, "when some hostess fears people will not attend her festivities, to send her servants out gossiping and spreading lies to excite curiosity."

"You make me feel like a flat. I had not heard of such a practice."

"My late wife, Clarissa, once created a sensation in Grosvenor Square by having it put about that she intended to display a two-headed monkey at her rout. There was no such animal, but silly society fought and pushed and screamed to get into my house. So determined were they to have a new piece of gossip that a remarkable amount of them claimed to have seen this monkey and even fed its two heads with nuts."

"So even if no one believes her to be a princess, they will insist she is until a better piece of tittle-tattle comes along?"

"Exactly."

"Perhaps this Miss Goodenough will turn out to be the bride for you," said Fitz, with a sidelong look at his friend's handsome face.

"Too young and too beautiful. I am looking for a lady of mature years, but not too old to bear children, and of good intelligence and dignity. If they are young, they are silly, and if they are beautiful, they are empty-headed and vain, having never had to make the least push to entertain."

"Are you not afraid that some of the house's notorious bad luck will stick to you?"

"Not I. I am not superstitious, but then, I am no gambler."

"It all looks very quiet," said Fitz as they turned the corner into Clarges Street. "No carriages, no crush."

"Then the princess tale has not taken," said the earl. "Society must be becoming more sophisticated. And I must be getting old. I am beginning to wish I had stayed quietly at home with a book. The relief of finding myself in comfortable surroundings after the noise of Limmer's Hotel makes me reluctant to go out anywhere."

"I wish you had stayed long enough at Limmer's to find out how that fellow, John Collins, makes that delicious gin concoction of his."

"Alas, no one yet has mastered his recipe, and so the only place you can find such a drink is at Limmer's. Here we are!"

Emily was beginning to feel faint with the strain of waiting.

She was a sitting on an an ornately carved gilt chair on a little raised dais in the front parlour. This throne-like effect had been created for her by Rainbird and Angus.

Her hair was dressed in one of the new Roman styles, with a fall of glossy ringlets from a knot at the back of her head and swept severely back at the front to show a tiara of diamonds and pearls to advantage.

Her gown was one she had bought in Bath. It had orginally been a modish cre-ation of oyster satin but had been embel-lished by a London dressmaker with pearl embroidery, which managed to make it look somewhat like a coronation gown. It had a square décolletage, cut daringly low to expose the top of her breasts. Her long silk gloves were clasped with "elastic" bracelets of pearl, the elasticity being supplied by small gold springs. Around her slim neck, she wore a collar of diamonds and pearls to match the tiara. Rundell & Bridge, the jewellers, had been delighted with the sale of the tiara and collar to Miss Goodenough, for with the current craze for cornelian, coral, amber, garnet, and jet, they had been wondering if they would ever sell another diamond again.

In a chair placed lower than Emily's "throne" sat Mrs. Middleton, her nose beginning to twitch with nerves.

Standing behind Emily, his hands behind his back, was Mr. Goodenough, looking more like a butler on duty than the master of the house.

"No one is coming," said Emily at last. "No one. Tell Rainbird to send the orchestra home, Mrs. Middleton."

With a sigh of pure relief, Mrs. Middleton got to her feet. But at the same time, Rainbird threw open the door and announced, "The Earl of Fleetwood and Mr. Jason Fitzgerald."

Mrs. Middleton collapsed back into her chair.

Fitz and the earl bowed before Emily, and then stood looking at her.

Emily looked back, wondering desperately whether princesses plunged into light chitter-chatter or whether they maintained a noble silence. She settled for silence.

Fitz was gazing with awe on Emily. It was rare to see such flawless, unpainted skin, such magnificent eyes, such a beauti-fully rounded bosom.

The earl began to look amused. He opened his mouth to say something to break the silence, and then closed it again, thinking it might be entertaining to see how long Miss Emily could maintain her role.

There was a loud pop as Rainbird opened a bottle of champagne, but Emily's beautiful eyes kept their fixed look.

Rainbird offered glasses of champagne to the earl and to Fitz. Fitz absent-mindedly took his glass without once removing his eyes from Emily's face.

The orchestra, consisting of four violinists and one elderly gentleman seated at a small spinet, were crammed into a corner of the back parlour behind a forest of hothouse flowers.

"Play!" hissed Rainbird, hoping to lighten the atmosphere.

The musicians began to play a slow, measured pavane that somehow seemed to intensify the silence between guests and hosts rather than dispel it.

Rainbird dashed down to the kitchen and seized Joseph, who was dressed in his best livery and about to go upstairs to take up his position. "Get your mandolin, Joseph," said Rainbird, "and play something bright and lively. Dave, get your best suit on and act as page. Alice and Jenny, you must act as footmen tonight."

"But it's as quiet as the grave up there!" cried Jenny.

"I feel in my bones that many people will be coming," said Rainbird. "Oh, hurry, Joseph, or Miss Emily will continue to sit there like a statue, and the gentlemen will take their leave!"

Giles, Lord Fleetwood's butler, decided to take his leave before he was pressed into service. Upstairs, Mrs. Middleton coughed genteelly and tried to think of something to say. Emily sat rigidly, looking straight ahead. She and Mrs. Middleton had decided earlier not to drink anything at all in case it dulled their wits. Now Emily longed for a glass of champagne but was frightened to say so. The earl's eyes were dancing wickedly but he made no sound. Fitz stood transfixed, like a man in a trance.

Mr. Goodenough was so unused to making any social conversation with anyone other than Emily that he remained quiet, feeling it was not his place to break the silence first.

Behind the dignified mask of her face, Emily was trembling with fright. She wondered if she would ever be able to speak again.

The Earl of Fleetwood looked devilish with his black, black hair and those slanting blue eyes. His evening dress was so exquisite, so faultless, so impeccable that he seemed twice as handsome as Emily had remembered, and twice as terrifying. And Mr. Fitzgerald was just as bad. Emily had never been so close to an Exquisite before. Fitz was so extravagantly dressed with his nipped-in waist, his embroidered waistcoat, and his huge starched shirt collar that he did not seem quite real to Emily. Mr. Fitzgerald's face, she noticed, was as highly painted as that of a female member of the Fashionable Impure. I am, thought Emily with an inward shudder, facing Decadence on the Hoof!

There was a noisy altercation in the back parlour and then the sombre music died away.

Lord Fleetwood was just deciding the fun had gone on long enough. It was time to bow and leave. Then the jaunty, dancing melody of a popular Italian song filled the room, with Joseph's sweet tenor singing the words.

A faint tinge of colour appeared on Emily's white cheeks and she smiled suddenly. The amused look left the earl's eyes and he stared at her, much as his friend had been staring at her.

"By Jove, that's a jolly tune," said Fitz.

"May I have some champagne, Rainbird?" asked Emily.

"I would like a glass as well," said Mrs. Middleton.

"I think I'll sit down," declared Mr. Goodenough. "What do you think, gentlemen? Will our new Prince Regent settle down, now he has attained the regency at last?"

Fitz crossed over to Mr. Goodenough's side and began to gossip. Emily took a glass of champagne and smiled again, shyly this time, at the earl. "I think I should like to walk about for a little," she said.

Emily promenaded up and down the small room with the earl while Mrs. Middleton fell into step behind her, anxious to correct any lapses in genteel speech if need be. But it was very hard to remain unobtrusive because of the very smallness of the room. Mrs. Middleton would no sooner get behind Emily and the earl than the couple would both turn and swing round, nearly colliding with her. Mrs. Middleton decided Emily appeared to be doing very nicely and so she retreated to a corner and sat down.

Mr. Goodenough was becoming quite animated as he discussed his hero, the Prince of Wales, who had only just been made regent. Fitz humoured Mr. Goodenough by listening politely to his praises of the prince, although he reflected cynically that the dissolute and greedy Prinny hardly deserved such accolades. Also, half Fitz's mind was occupied in wondering what the earl was saying to Emily.

"You appear to be lucky in your chef," said the earl to Emily as they swung about to traverse the room for the sixth time. "There are some delicious smells arising from the kitchen."

"He is very good indeed," said Emily. "Not only with French dishes, but with our traditional English ones. His sirloin of beef is done to a cow's thumb."

"Indeed!" said the earl, startled at the common expression which had dropped so gently from Miss Emily's pink lips.

Rainbird passed with a tray of glasses of champagne. Emily put her empty glass on the tray, took a full one, and drained it in one gulp. "I was very thirsty," she said apologetically, remembering too late she was supposed to sip it.

"It is a problem finding a genuine French chef," said the earl. "So many of them claim to be French who have never been south of Dover."

"MacGregor, the cook, is Scotch," said Emily, "but a real treasure and not a bale of flat cater traes. I mean," she explained with a deep blush, "that he is genuinely a good chef and not . . ."

"Like false dice," said the earl, completing her explanation. "I am well versed in cant, Miss Goodenough, but I am surprised that *you* are so well acquainted with it. Do you plan to bring it into fashion?"

Emily took a deep breath and decided to

lie. She was already acting a lie. What would one more falsehood matter?

"You must forgive me, my lord," she said. "English is not my first language."

She looked up into his eyes as she spoke and saw little imps of mischief dancing in them as those blue eyes of his looked down into her own.

"You are fortunate, Miss Goodenough," said the earl, "for I speak many foreign languages. In which one would you like to converse?"

Emily looked at him miserably wondering what to say, but she was saved by Rainbird, who threw open the door to the front parlour and began to announce new arrivals.

They came in droves, pushing and shoving to get in, apologising for being late, the ladies lisping and cooing and the men bowing, waving lace handkerchiefs, and flicking little snuff-boxes open.

The earl backed away as Emily was surrounded by eager and curious London society.

Emily found she was not expected to say anything but merely to listen and smile. Joseph's jaunty music continued to liven the rooms of the thin house, which was slowly being crammed with people.

The earl caught Fitz's eye and signalled they should take their leave. Emily had retreated to her throne and was holding court as men and women clustered around her. Then, just as the earl was edging his way through the press to make his farewells, one excitable young miss waved her glass in the air and half the contents went over Emily's gown and the other half on the breeches on Lord Agnesby, an elderly fop who was standing next to Emily.

Emily dabbed at the spilled champagne on her gown with a handkerchief and said mournfully in her clear, carrying voice, "Dear me, I am soaked through to my dicky." There was a startled, shocked silence, for to refer to one's petticoat as a dicky was to use the lowest possible form of slang.

Trying to cover up her obvious gaffe, Emily made matters worse by turning to Lord Agnesby and saying, "I trust your breeches are not ruined."

There was an indrawn hiss. *No* lady ever let that word "breeches" fall from her lips. She might coyly refer to them as inexpressibles but never by any other name.

Emily's social future hung in the balance.

Then into the silence came the Earl of

Fleetwood's pleasant husky voice. "Your Royal Highness," he began. Then he started and appeared to collect himself. "I beg your pardon, I mean Miss Goodenough. Mr. Fitzgerald and I wish to thank you for a handsome entertainment. I shall call on Your . . . on you tomorrow in the hope I can persuade you to come driving with me."

There was a little excited fluttering and whispering about him. One young lady hissed excitedly to her friend, "I *told* you she was a princess. After all, our dear Princess Charlotte talks as if she had lived all her life in a stable!"

The earl and Fitz bowed and withdrew. It took them quite ten minutes to fight their way out.

"Whew!" said Fitz, mopping his brow after they had walked a little way away from the house. "You saved her. You certainly saved her. What an angel, but what language! Who do you think she really is?"

"I don't know," said the earl thoughtfully. "But I mean to find out!"

Emily thought her guests would never leave. She smiled until her face felt stiff. She was deeply grateful to Mrs. Middleton, who, enlivened by several glasses of champagne, was talking away with great panache, and fielding all the questions thrown at Emily like a social expert.

Emily managed to murmur to Rainbird that she was anxious for the evening to be over.

Rainbird retired to the back parlour, told Joseph to stop playing, and the sulky orchestra that it might resume its labours.

The orchestra began where it had left off with that dreary pavane. As steady as a dead march, the measured notes fell on the guests' ears.

It is only the right music that can soothe the savage breast and lie sweetly on the spirit. The orchestra's selection was like a death's head—slow and mournful notes to remind society of the futility of life and the instability of the spleen.

At first they began to leave in ones and twos and then in great groups. There were a few gentlemen who seemed determined to worship at the shrine of Emily's beauty forever, but when Rainbird stopped passing around with glasses of wine and champagne, it occurred to them that the night was still young and that Emily could be worshipped just as easily on the morrow. Soon the last carriage had rolled off down Clarges Street.

Emily and Mr. Goodenough retired to a corner of the dining room upstairs and left the servants to clear up the mess, Emily wondering if she would ever get used to being waited on.

"Well, that went very well, my dear," said Mr. Goodenough. "But it might have turned out to be a disaster had not the Earl of Fleetwood stepped in. You do have an awful tongue, Emily. And you should have warned me you meant to pass yourself off as a princess."

"I know," said Emily. "I should be grateful to Fleetwood, but there is something about that man which frightens me. I sometimes suspect he knows exactly who I am and is laughing at me, and, yes, laughing at society at the same time for being such fools as to believe my story."

"You cannot hope to marry an earl," said Mr. Goodenough with a little sigh. "It is not likely you will see him again. He did not seem very much interested in you and only stayed for a little."

"Why cannot I marry an earl?" asked Emily curiously, although she herself had never thought such a thing possible. "When we first hit on this plan for a Season in London, you said I could marry a duke."

"We are dreamers," said Mr. Good-enough. "But even dreamers such as we must face reality. It is not just because Fleetwood is an earl, it is because he is a very *rich* earl. Should, say, he propose to you, then I should be confronted by a battery of his lawyers, all firing questions at me, talking about marriage settlements, and demanding particulars of your ancestry. No, no. A poor gentleman—well, not too well-heeled—is what you require. A poor gentleman's lawyers, if he can afford any, are not going to disaffect a good parti with probing questions."

"Then it is as well Fleetwood does not interest me." Emily laughed. "What is this business about this house being unlucky?"

"Ah, we should have known there was a reason for the low rent. I gathered from various guests that all sorts of frightening things have gone on under this roof: a beautiful girl murdered, her murderer unmasked while trying to kill one of the tenants, a family ruined, and even a dreadful suicide."

"What was the dreadful suicide?" asked Emily faintly.

"That of the former Duke of Pelham."

"Merciful heavens! I am surprised anyone dared to call!"

"Oh, they felt the bad luck only applied to those who live here. I do not believe in such stuff and nonsense. Do you?"

"No," said Emily stoutly.

But when she went to bed that night, she asked Joseph to light the way upstairs, and lay awake for quite a long time, watching the patterns made by the rushlight on the ceiling, and remembering that mischievous mocking look in the earl's eyes.

"Trouble is coming," thought Emily with a shiver. "I can feel it!"

# Chapter Six

*Come to our fête, and bring with thee*
*Thy newest, best embroidery!*
*Come to our fête, and show again*
*That pea-green coat, thou pink of men!*
*Which charmed all eyes, that last sur-*
*    veyed it;*
*When Brummel's self inquired "who*
*    made it?"*
                    —Thomas Moore

"And how was your drive in the Park with the fair princess?" asked Fitz the following evening as both gentlemen with their bicornes and canes tucked under their arms made their way to the opera.

"I did not have an opportunity to take Miss Goodenough driving. Her drawing room was packed with curious society, all content to stare at her as if she were a freak at Bartholomew Fair. I presented my compliments, promised to call again when I should find her not so besieged, and took my leave," said the earl.

"She must be enjoying all the attention."

"Not she," said the earl, tossing a coin to a crossing sweeper. "She remained calm and stately, but at the back of her eyes was a flicker of fear. Our princess is not only not a princess but, I should think, of quite common clay. That uncle of hers looks as if he should be a servant rather than a gentleman."

"Come now! You are too harsh. I found Mr. Goodenough very gentlemanly."

"But there is a deference there, a whole attitude of *service*. It is hard to explain."

"Perhaps Miss Goodenough *is* a princess. That would explain her unease and her odd English."

"She did try to tell me English was not her first language. I do not believe it. Now, our young ladies of the ton affect to be shy and timid and to have excessive sensibility, but you can tell from their eyes that they know their station in life and know what is due to them. This afternoon, I intercepted several glances cast by the fair Emily in the direction of her butler, glances of appeal between equals. Yes, I think I shall find Miss Goodenough is an adventuress."

"Is that such a terrible crime? Society

abounds with opportunists, and most of them not half so pretty."

"Not a crime in my eyes, unless she proves to be a servant who has run off with her mistress's dresses and jewels. Low origins are one thing, servants another. When Clarissa was found dead, that staff of mine tattled and gossiped fit to beat the band."

"You must often wonder who actually killed your poor wife."

The earl's face wore a closed, hard look. Then he said, "Let us talk of better things. My book will be out next week. Do you think I shall be savaged in the *Edinburgh Review?*"

"Only if you have pilloried the reviewer," said Fitz.

Both men preferred to be unfashionable and walk to Covent Garden, neither seeing the point in spending hours in a crush of carriages, waiting to be set down outside the opera house.

On their arrival, they found that the famous Catalini, who was billed to sing that evening, was unwell and had been replaced by a minor diva.

"There will be so much noise," said the earl, "it is hardly worthwhile going in."

"What an odd creature you are!" said

Fitz with a laugh. "You must be the only person in London who goes to the opera to hear the music. Everyone else goes to be seen. Come along. I have this new coat which has not yet had a chance to stun society."

"If your shoulders become more padded and your collars any higher," said the earl drily, "they will begin to take you for a headless man. Besides, a noisy opera house always generates heat, and heat makes your rouge melt."

"I have a becoming colour," said Fitz stiffly.

"You are not going to tell me that noisy sunset across your cheeks is your own!"

"It is helped a little, that is all."

"My dear friend, I can dimly remember the days when you were well-scrubbed. Your face is not pock-marked, nor is it sallow. Why the desire to wear so much paint?"

But Fitz could not explain. Since his injury had left him feeling like half a man, he had become a peacock. The pain in his back seemed bearable when he was dressed in the extremes of fashion, as if the mask of fashion briefly turned him into someone else.

The opera house was already crowded when they entered. The prostitutes were doing a roaring trade in the centre boxes, and the bucks in the pit were buying oranges to hurl at Catalini's substitute.

"There is your princess," said Fitz.

Emily sat in a side box, with Mrs. Middleton beside her and Mr. Goodenough dozing in a chair at the back. People began to enter her box and soon she was blocked from their view.

"Poor girl," said Fitz. "She is still society's latest interest. Can she stand the pace, think you?"

"She is very young," said the earl. "She has, despite her coarse speech, a great amount of sensibility. I should think she is already under a great strain."

"The days of knight-errantry are gone," said Fitz, shaking his head. "We should create a diversion, something that will make society focus on something else."

The orchestra struck the opening chords of the overture to the opera. The crowd about Emily left. She sat there, in the blazing light cast by the huge overhead chandelier, her face very white, her hands shredding a handkerchief in her lap.

The earl raised his quizzing glass and studied her. He barely knew her; he was sure no woman could hold any fascination for him merely because she was beautiful. But as he watched her, he felt a pang of compassion, an odd longing to shield her from the consequences of what he was convinced was her own folly.

He muttered something under his breath, rose to his feet, and left the box.

The earl was subsequently seen visiting box after box, finally ending up bowing before Emily. Fitz wondered what on earth his friend was up to. The noise from the pit grew louder and harsher. The diva on the stage was becoming very angry and was hurling the missiles thrown at her back at the audience. This was considered highly sporting of her, and after a little more shouting and noise the audience decided to give her a chance and settled down to listen.

The earl returned during the interval. "Come, Fitz," he said. "We have much to do. I am giving a rout—an impromptu rout at midnight."

"But everyone will stay for the ball after the opera! No one will come."

"Oh, yes they will. All declare themselves anxious to make the acquaintance of London's latest star—Princess Anastasia Moussepof."

"Never heard of her. Who is she?"

"You, my dear chap. You."

"Do you really think I should attend Fleetwood's rout?" Emily asked Mrs. Middleton.

"I think it would be wise, Miss Goodenough. Fleetwood is admired by all. The Prince Regent himself might come, if he hears of it."

"Then we *must* go," cried Mr. Goodenough. "I have long been an admirer of the Prince Regent, and it has always been my dream to meet him."

"But I fear Fleetwood may be mocking us," said Emily anxiously. "Another princess! He had that funny droll look in his eyes when he issued the invitation. I am so weary of being thought a princess. Unless something happens to divert society's attention from me, then someone is going to become over-curious and unmask me."

"Perhaps this new princess will be just the thing," said Mrs. Middleton.

"But what if I am introduced to her as another princess and *she* starts questioning me?"

"Then you must do what you have done with everyone else," said Mrs. Middleton. "Deny that you are a princess. So far, no one seems to have believed you, but perhaps when they hear you tell this Princess Anastasia so, then they will come to accept you as Miss Goodenough. But you must admit, it *was* a good idea. You would not have met anyone in society had it not been for Lizzie's idea."

"Who is Lizzie?"

"The little scullery maid. A most superior person. Shhh! The opera is about to recommence."

Emily barely heard any of it. She felt the strain of being an impostor. It was bad enough being an ex-chambermaid—but to pretend to be a princess! Only the other week, some unfortunate had been hanged outside Newgate for pretending to be a peer of the realm. But that was an *English* peer. They surely could not hang someone for pretending to be *a foreign* princess. Why did Fleetwood look at her with that mocking, amused expression in his eyes?

Poor Emily's worries went on and on while the undistinguished opera by a little-known Italian composer dragged on to the end. The opera was followed by a farce, and then it was time to go to the Earl of Fleetwood's house in Park Lane.

As they left the opera house, Emily glanced at herself in one of the long mirrors.

A beautiful and elegant lady looked back. "If only I could feel like a lady *inside*," mourned Emily.

On the way to Park Lane in their rented carriage, with the tall figure of Joseph clinging to the backstrap, each occupant was immersed in his and her private thoughts. Emily was deciding that it would be a relief, in a way, to be unmasked. This Season had been a great mistake. How could she have ever dreamt of marriage to one of *them?* Better to retire to the country with her dear friend and live a quiet and comfortable existence. God put us in our appointed stations the day we were born, and to try to move up or down was a heinous sin.

Mr. Goodenough was praying that the Prince Regent would be there. If only he could make his bow, and look on those famous features, he felt he would die a happy man.

Mrs. Middleton was deathly tired. She hoped they would only stay a short time at the rout. Her feet were swelling inside her new shoes, and her new corset was pinching her above the waist. Emily had not uttered one coarse phrase during all the socialising before the opera began. Mrs. Middleton had enjoyed her brief elevation to the ranks of society, but now all she wanted to do was to get back to her comfortable parlour and become a housekeeper again.

The earl's house was a blaze of lights from top to bottom. The Goodenoughs and Mrs. Middleton had to wait and wait while their carriage inched forward through the press.

When they finally alighted, Emily called Joseph and told him to accompany them inside. She was quickly coming to rely more and more on the Clarges Street servants and felt Joseph's tall presence behind her at the rout would be a comfort.

Joseph was thrilled at the idea of having a look at a real-live princess. It almost took his mind off his nagging worry about Lizzie and why Luke should suddenly have become interested in her.

The first thing Emily noticed was that there were no refreshments, no cards, no music. She blushed as she thought of her own efforts and wondered whether she had been considered parvenu to have supplied food, drink, and an orchestra.

Emily, Mr. Goodenough, Mrs. Middleton, and Joseph queued on the staircase that led up to the drawing room on the first floor.

There was a great deal of pushing and shoving as some members of the ton shoved their way up and others who had had the glory of meeting the princess pushed their way down.

At last, Emily's party reached the double doors of the drawing room.

Mr. Goodenough scrambled for his card case, could not find it, and gave their names in a shaky voice.

The little party walked forward.

Emily's heart sank.

For here, surely, was a real princess.

She was a tall, elegant lady wearing an enormous powdered wig. Her face was a mask of white blanc with a circle of rouge painted on each cheek. She was wearing a long, flowing, crimson velvet robe heavily encrusted with gold embroidery. Heavy barbaric necklaces of huge rubies and sapphires set in old gold hung about her neck and fell almost to her waist over her flat bosom.

The earl was standing behind her chair.

"And who is this?" demanded the princess in a surprisingly deep voice.

"Miss Emily Goodenough," murmured the earl, "her uncle, Mr. Benjamin Goodenough, and Miss Emily's companion, Mrs. Middleton."

"You are very beautiful, child," said the princess. "You may kiss me."

Emily shyly walked forward, sank into a deep curtsy, and then made to kiss the princess on the cheek. She found herself seized in a strong grip and then, to her consternation, the princess kissed her full on the mouth.

"I should call you out for that, you old ratbag," said the earl.

Blushing furiously, Emily retreated backwards and looked at the earl and the princess in surprise.

Mr. Goodenough made his bow and Mrs. Middleton dropped her best curtsy.

Just as they were about to leave, there came a great stirring and rustling and exclaiming from those waiting to be presented, and then Giles called out, "His Royal Highness, the Prince Regent; Mr. George Brummell; Lord Alvanley."

"The deuce!" exclaimed the earl.

The Prince Regent waddled forward. He was wearing skin-tight knee-breeches and his evening coat was strained across his shoulders. Slim, elegant, and amused, the famous Beau Brummell stood behind him with the squat and powerful Lord Alvanley.

"Princess Anastasia," said the prince, "we

are delighted to welcome you to our country."

The princess stood up and dropped an awkward curtsy.

"We were not informed of your arrival by your ambassador," pursued the prince.

"My regrets," murmured the princess.

"He being the ambassador of . . . ?" The prince looked enquiringly at the princess, who looked wildly to the earl for support.

"I am afraid, Your Royal Highness," said the earl, "that our princess is . . ." He reached forward and lifted the wig from Princess Anastasia's head. "None other than Mr. Jason Fitzgerald, at your service."

Fitz bowed from the waist. The Prince Regent gazed at him, outraged.

Then, from behind them, Emily began to laugh. It was a clear, ringing, infectious laugh. The prince turned about and surveyed her. She was holding her sides and laughing whole-heartedly.

"Gad's 'oonds!" cried the prince. "You devil, Fleetwood." He began to laugh as well. Everyone began to laugh helplessly, and those that did not know what the prince was laughing at, for they were still jammed out on the staircase, nonetheless began to laugh as well. For if something amused the

Prince Regent, then it followed that everyone else *must* be amused, whether they knew the joke or not.

"Who is this?" demanded the prince, when he had finished laughing, looking at Emily.

"May I present London's famous beauty," said the earl, "Miss Emily Goodenough." He looked to where Mr. Goodenough stood behind Emily, trembling with hope and excitement. "And her uncle, Mr. Goodenough, and her companion, Mrs. Middleton."

Emily, despite her beauty, was forgotten as the prince looked at the shaking awe and admiration on Mr. Goodenough's twisted face.

His portly chest swelled. He extended two podgy fingers. "We are pleased to make your acquaintance, Mr. Goodenough," he said.

White with excitement, Mr. Goodenough shook those royal fingers. "Your Royal Highness," he gasped, "I shall treasure this moment until the day I die."

"Tol rol," said the prince, waving a dismissive hand, but looking vastly pleased. "And Mrs. Middleton, is it not? Charmed."

Mrs. Middleton looked at him with hero-worship in her eyes.

Becoming more pleased by the minute, the prince chucked Emily under the chin. "Indeed a beauty," he said. "Going to snatch her up, hey, Fleetwood?"

"If Miss Goodenough will give me a chance to do so," said the earl smoothly. "Giles! Champagne for His Highness, if you please."

The laughing crowd moved around the prince and cut him off from Emily's view.

Emily stood stunned. She had met the Prince Regent! What was more important, Mr. Goodenough had met the Prince Regent. Surely they needed nothing more from this Season.

Voices rose and fell about her. "We shall have to plan something different for *our* rout," said one. "Princesses are quite exploded, my dear. I suppose that Miss Goodenough was playing a joke on us as well. Still, now she has Prinny's favour, she can do no wrong. I never thought she was a princess anyway."

"But she is high ton," said another voice, "or Fleetwood would never have proposed to her in front of the prince."

"He never did!"

"Not in so many words, but that is what he implied. And Fleetwood is a very high

110

stickler. Goodenough. Never heard of them. Must hail from the untitled aristocracy."

Emily heaved a sigh of relief. At least she did not have to pretend to be a princess any more.

She signalled to a dazed Mrs. Middleton that they should take their leave.

Joseph followed them down the staircase, muttering, "Oh, my! Oh, my! Wait until I tell Rainbird. Our own Mrs. Middleton meeting the prince. Oh, my!"

Joseph could hardly wait to get to the servants' hall to tell everyone the news. But Emily, elated and delighted that her role as princess was over, summoned the staff into the front parlour and asked Rainbird to serve them all champagne.

"I am behaving in a very common way," she thought, "by entertaining servants, but I am tired of being a lady. From now on I am going to be myself."

And in all the relief and excitement, Emily forgot she was still an adventuress, still an impostor, and that, if society ever found out she was an ex-chambermaid, they would hound her out of Town.

# Chapter Seven

*We missed you last night at the "hoary old
    sinners,"*
*Who gave us, as usual, the cream of good
    dinners—*
*His soups scientific—his fishes quite* prime—
*His pâtés superb—and his cutlets sublime!*
*In short, 'twas the snug sort of dinner to stir a*
*Stomachic orgasm in my Lord Ellenborough,*
*Who* set to, *to be sure, with miraculous
    force,*
*And exclaimed, between mouthfuls, "A
    He-Cook, of course!—*
*While you live—(What's that under that
    cover, Pray, look)—*
*While you live—(I'll just taste it)—ne'er keep
    a She-Cook,*
*'Tis a sound Sallic Law—(a small bit of that
    toast)—*
*Which ordains that a female shall ne'er rule
    the roast;*
*For Cookery's a secret—(this turtle's un-
    common)—*

*Like Masonry, never found out by a woman!"*

—Thomas Moore

In the week that followed, Lord Fleetwood did not call. Emily tried to tell herself she was relieved, although he had—unwittingly, she was sure—saved her from having to maintain her pose as a princess. She had many beaux and plenty of invitations. She and Mr. Goodenough decided to relax and enjoy a little more of the Season before deciding what to do next. Emily had more or less made up her mind *not* to find a husband, and that decision had made life easier. She made no more slips into common speech and soon found she was able to converse naturally without guarding her tongue every minute.

It was Lizzie, Lizzie the scullery maid, of all people, who shattered Emily's equanimity. It was part of Lizzie's duties to wash down the stairs and keep the doorstep outside whitened with pipe clay.

So one afternoon, just as Emily was leaving, escorted by Joseph, to go and potter about the shops in Oxford Street, she came across Lizzie, who was dreamily pipe-claying the front steps while she read a book, spread open on the steps in front of her.

Lizzie jumped to her feet and bobbed a curtsy.

"You seem to be enjoying that book," said Emily with a smile. "Who wrote it?"

"It doesn't say, ma'am," said Lizzie. "It only says 'by A Gentleman.' It's ever so funny but a bit crool."

"Cruel? How so?"

"Well, the main character is this chambermaid called Emilia, who steals her mistress's jewels and takes herself off to London, where she pretends to be a lady and trick this lord into marriage. He first becomes suspicious when he begins to notice a certain coarseness in her speech, and—"

"Thank you," said Emily stiffly. "Return to your work."

She swept off down Clarges Street, with Joseph behind her.

Joseph found he was having to trot to keep up with her. Emily felt confused and frightened. It did not dawn on her that a writer could hardly have managed to use her for a model for one of the characters in his book and get it published, all in the short time she had been in London. She felt that someone in society had pierced her disguise and was sitting somewhere watching her, like a cat watching a mouse.

But by the time she reached Oxford Street, her panic was dying down. It was a coincidence, that was all. She, Emily, had not stolen anything. She would go to Hatchard's in Piccadilly and buy a copy of the book and prove to herself that all her worries were over nothing. Joseph groaned inwardly and wondered at this sudden decision to go back to Piccadilly, when they could easily have gone there in the first place.

At Hatchard's, Emily was told the book was sold out. Although she did not know the title, the bookseller assured her that there was only one book out by 'A Gentleman' and that it was called *Above Her Station* or *The Vain Folly of a Presumptuous Servant*.

Emily returned to Clarges Street. As she rounded the corner from the Piccadilly end, she heard a stifled exclamation from Joseph, but assumed his feet were hurting as usual. Joseph always wore shoes two sizes too small for him. He was not alone in this folly. Small feet were considered aristocratic, and there were many bent and twisted toes and fallen arches in London to bear witness to the fact that a surprising number of people were prepared to suffer in the name of vanity. But it was the sight of Luke, leaning casually against the railings of Number 67 and talking to Lizzie, which had caused Joseph to exclaim.

Luke saw them approach, said something to Lizzie, and then darted off down the area steps of Number 65.

Emily saw the book now lying closed at the side of the steps.

"May I borrow your book?" she asked Lizzie when she came up to her.

"Certainly, ma'am," said Lizzie, dropping a curtsy. "It's not really *my* book, being as how we club together when we all want to read a new book. Mostly, we buy them second-hand."

She handed Emily the book. Emily murmured her thanks. She brushed past Rainbird, who was holding open the door, and walked quickly upstairs, clutching the book. Rainbird looked after her in surprise. It was unlike Miss Emily to walk past without so much as a smile or a "good day."

Emily tore off her bonnet and then sat down in a chair by the window and began to read.

The maid in the book, Emilia, had dark-brown hair and blue-grey eyes, just like

Emily. She was aided and abetted in the theft of her mistress's jewels by the butler—"a man whose twisted and sinister face betrayed his low character." With a sinking heart, Emily read on. In the author's opinion, a member of the servant class must always betray herself. Low origins and common blood will always unmask the impostor. Not only was this Emilia portrayed as a beautiful girl with the heart of a conniving slut, but all the servants in the book were described as being greedy, gossiping, talebearing monsters. The fact that the author was equally acid about the posing and double standards of society escaped Emily's terrified eyes. Emilia's lusty, earthy passions were also held up as an example of her low origins. The author appeared to assume that ladies did not feel any urgings of the flesh.

But Emily did. All her romantic yearnings and her sometimes shocking dreams now appeared to her as an example of the whole unladylikeness of her character. Ladies, it appeared, married to increase the fortune of some man and bear his children. Women at the mercy of their passions belonged to the lower orders or to the Fashionable Impure.

Rainbird scratched at the door from time

to time to say there was this or that gentle-man waiting below to present his compli-ments, but Emily replied each time that she had a headache. She did not want to leave the room until she had studied the book thoroughly.

The book was quite short, only one vol-ume, unlike most novels, which ran to at least three, but Emily read it slowly and carefully.

By the time she had finished it, she became convinced someone knew about her and Mr. Goodenough. She crossed to the window, as if dreading to see a mocking face watching the house.

She wondered whether to take the book to Mr. Goodenough, and then decided against it. She must bear the burden of this worry alone. Mr. Goodenough was not strong. Since his apoplexy, he tired easily.

Then the mocking eyes of the Earl of Fleetwood seemed to look back at her. The gentlemen who called on her were whole-hearted in their adoration. Only the earl had looked at her as if there were something about her that amused him.

And he had not called!

All at once, Emily wanted to see him again, to reassure herself that there was no one in London who had pierced her mask, and that a book about an ex-chambermaid fobbing herself off on London society as a lady was a coincidence.

But *how* to see him again? Of course if she continued to attend the many society functions to which she had been invited, then she was bound to run into him, but anxious Emily felt she could not wait.

The earl had given an impromptu rout. Then she, Emily, would give an impromptu dinner. She pulled forward a sheet of paper, sharpened a quill, and started to make out a list of names, including that of the Earl of Fleetwood.

"Our new beauty seems very confident of her power," said Lord Fleetwood the next day as Fitz strolled into his drawing room. "I am summoned to an impromptu dinner tomorrow evening."

"And I," said Fitz. "I shall most certainly attend. What about you?"

"Yes, I think it might be amusing. Good heavens, Fritz. You are clean!"

"I am usually clean," said Fitz, very stiffly on his stiffs.

"But, my dear chap, not a trace of paint!

119

And the shoulders of your coat are of a normal height."

Fitz gave a rueful grin. "Dressing up as that princess cured me of the extravagances of fashion. My valet now boasts the highest collars and the most padded coats in London."

"You look quite human. It will take me some time to get accustomed to the new Fitz."

"It was partly because you chose to mock me in your book. I recognized myself in Lord Fopworthy."

"I would never dream of ridiculing you! Alas! Everyone recognises himself or herself in my book. But I assure you, all the characters came out of my imagination and are not based on any individual I know."

"But no one believes that! And all are speculating as to the identity of the maid, Emilia."

"They will have something else to speculate about very shortly."

"And what are you going to do to celebrate your earnings from your work of fiction? Give a party?"

"Not I. I have sent the initial money to the workhouse at Tothill Fields with instructions it is to be used to improve the diet of the inmates."

"You are naïve. The money will disappear into the pockets of the board."

"They would not dare. They know I have a nasty habit of making surprise visits. I have even had to go in disguise, for when I sent them the proceeds of my first book, they posted a small boy at the corner of the street to warn the workhouse of my coming, and the inmates were given good food only for the length of my visit. Fortunately, a man in the workhouse proved to be literate and contrived to send me a letter telling me of what was taking place. He is now one of my grooms, although I confess I left him in the workhouse for a certain length of time until I found my instructions were being followed."

"I did not know you were a philanthropist," said Fitz awkwardly. "I mean, it is all very worthy of you, but not very realistic. These people choose to be poor, and too much meat puts revolutionary ideas into their heads. Had it not been for the well-fed bourgeoisie of France, there never would have been a revolution. The peasants were too hungry to think of anything but their next meal."

"Fitz, you are talking fustian."

"Not I," said Fitz stubbornly. "People are put in their appointed stations the day they are born. You are quarrelling with the Almighty. After all, in your book you held that chambermaid up to ridicule. It was an example to everyone of what can happen to someone of the common lot who tries to climb."

"You know, Fitz, you have perhaps persuaded me of a fact I knew all along—I have written a thoroughly silly book. I am not a writer. I am a sort of literary dilettante, nothing more. I had great fun writing it and it all seemed amusing at the time, but I confess when I reread it the other day, I felt I was reading one of those embarrassingly trivial works written by some member of society with more vanity than talent."

"But it was monstrous amusing! All London is already talking of your satire of Byron."

"There you go again! I did not even *think* of Byron. Never mind my stupid book. I would rather think of Miss Goodenough."

"You all but proposed to her in front of Prinny."

"I do not know why I said that," remarked the earl ruefully. "I was somewhat overset and she appeared very . . . lovable."

"But *you* would not be satisfied with mere beauty. Say you married her. You could never bear her vulgarisms."

"I think she has a good heart."

"Have you heard from your brother Harry?"

"What on earth has my brother to do with Miss Goodenough?"

"I suddenly thought of him. He was always desperately in love with some female or another."

"No, I have not heard from him. As far as I know, he is still a captain in the Eighty-seventh Dragoons, and no doubt preparing to fall in love with every Spanish señorita he encounters in the Peninsula."

"I am meeting some fellows for a rubber at White's. Do you care to come?"

"Not I. The excitement of dinner with Miss Goodenough will be enough for one day," said the earl.

Fitz took his leave, only to have his place taken shortly afterwards by the earl's sister, Mrs. Otterley. The earl heartily wished he had escaped with Fitz before her arrival.

"To what do I owe the pleasure of this visit?" asked the earl, thinking for the umpteenth time how nasty and bad-tempered his sister always looked.

"Scandal," said Mrs. Otterley, plumping her heavy bulk in a Sheraton chair. "I hear you proposed marriage to an Unknown."

"I gave a rout, I made a joke, that was all that happened."

"Not the way I heard it," sniffed Mrs. Otterley. "Some female called Goodenough was the recipient of your attentions. Pray remember what is due to your name before you throw yourself away on a Nobody. No one has ever heard of this creature before this Season."

"Should I marry again, then I will consult only myself, Mary. If that's what you had come to say, and now you have said it, please go away."

"She cannot have much money, this Miss Goodenough," went on Mrs. Otterley, who had a hide like a rhinoceros. "Else why would she have taken that unlucky house in Clarges Street? It is well known the only way it can ever be let is by charging a ridiculously low rent."

"I am not interested in money. I have enough."

"Too much for your own good," said his sister sharply.

Some imp of malice prompted the earl to say, "You know, Mary, Miss Goodenough *is* out of the common way. I could do worse than marry her. And I would need my home in Grosvenor Square back. You can always live here."

"But this is not nearly such a fashionable address!"

"Nonsense. We are come up in the world. Park Lane is all that is respectable. If you are so concerned about appearances, why do you not use your title?"

"You know very well that Mr. Otterley prefers me to carry his name."

"And my dear brother-in-law is so very rich, you needs must obey. And yet *his* pride does not stop him from living on *my* property. I grow stubborn, Mary. Your visit has only served to remind me that I should not be obliged to rent a house for the Season when I have a very good one of my own. I am sure Miss Goodenough will share your views. She would infinitely prefer Grosvenor Square to Park Lane."

"You are funning. All this marriage business is a joke. You are only trying to irritate me!"

"And succeeding very well . . . I hope,"

said her brother. "Do please leave, Mary, or I shall have a spasm."

But it was Mrs. Otterley who seemed more likely to have a spasm as she stormed out into Park Street—nothing would induce her to set foot in Park Lane, which she considered a very parvenu sort of thoroughfare.

She told her driver to proceed to Clarges Street.

Soon Rainbird was announcing the arrival of Lady Mary Powell. This was one occasion on which Mrs. Otterley was determined to use her title.

Emily was arranging spring flowers in the drawing-room when Mrs. Otterley was ushered in. She asked her pugnacious visitor to be seated. Mrs. Otterley waited impatiently until Rainbird had served her with a glass of cordial and had withdrawn before she launched into the attack.

"I have just heard, Miss Goodenough," she said, "that my brother is intent on proposing marriage to you."

"Your brother . . . ?"

"Fleetwood."

"He made some remark at his rout," said Emily, "but I assure you it was in jest and I have not seen him since."

126

Mrs. Otterley drained her cordial in one noisy gulp, clutched her enormous reticule on her lap, and glared at Emily with a hard, penetrating stare, as if she hoped some of the power of her look would wither a little of the girl's startling beauty.

"I hope you are right," she said. "For your sake, for your life, I hope you are right."

Emily had taken a hearty dislike to the lady. "Are you threatening me?" she asked.

"Good heavens, no!" Mrs. Otterley tried to force out a jolly laugh, but it sounded as happy as the noise of a rusty gate creaking in a high wind on a winter's night. "My brother is a very jealous man and has a dangerously unstable temper. Alas, poor Clarissa!"

Emily compressed her soft lips into a firm line and refused to ask who this Clarissa was.

"Fleetwood's wife," said Mrs. Otterley, just as if she *had* asked. "Found beaten to death. Fleetwood was lucky he did not hang."

"Are you telling me that Lord Fleetwood, your own brother, is a murderer?"

"Now, I did not say that," said Mrs.

Otterley. "I am here to tell you what other people are saying."

But Emily's servant background had made her less gullible than the young lady in whom Lord Fleetwood had shown an interest in the previous Season.

As a chambermaid, and while her master still was well enough to entertain, she had heard much malicious gossip, most of it untrue, concocted by ladies and gentlemen who appeared to think a servant was deaf. She decided she did not like the earl's sister one little bit.

Emily cast a dazzling smile on her. "My dear Lady Mary," she said with a rippling laugh, "I was afraid you were about to tell me your brother's wife was still *alive!* What a relief. Now I can accept his proposal with an easy heart."

"But you said he had no interest in you!"

Emily took a deep breath. In the space of a few seconds she decided she would never be frightened of any member of society again. She was *weary* of being frightened. They were just *people*, some pleasant, and some, like Mrs. Otterley, nasty.

"I was joking," said Emily. She rang the bell. "Good day to you, my lady. I doubt if we shall meet again . . . unless, of

128

course, Fleetwood wishes you to attend the wedding."

Mrs. Otterley opened and shut her mouth like a landed carp.

This young woman, who had looked so guileless, and, yes, timid when Mrs. Otterley had entered the room, now looked as contemptuously amused as Fleetwood at his worst.

Rainbird appeared in the doorway. "My lady is leaving," said Emily. "Show her out."

Mrs. Otterley hated to leave a scene without having the last word. She was determined not to leave this one. She huffed and puffed, her figure swelled, her eyes bulged as she summoned up all her energies to deliver a set-down.

But Mrs. Otterley's parsimony was her downfall. Like many of the aristocracy, she had her little meannesses. Some would not give a coin to a crossing sweeper and would rather soil their shoes in the mud, others watered the wine, still more kept their lady's maids working day and night turning last year's fashions into this year's creations. Mrs. Otterley was mean about corsets. The whalebone monster, which had encased her girth—unchanged, like the corset, since her wedding day—at first creaked ominously under the strain. Then one whalebone stay sprang from its threadbare moorings and stabbed straight into Mrs. Otterley's left-hand, floppy, saggy bosom.

Her face turned puce and then white. The only way she could alleviate the dreadful pain was by taking the pierced bosom and pushing it up with both hands. She tried to speak, but the indignity she was suffering was too great. Holding her great breast in both hands as if she were holding a pudding, Mrs. Otterley rushed out.

"Is that an insult, Rainbird?" Emily asked the butler after he had closed the street door behind Mrs. Otterley and returned.

"An insult, miss?"

"Well, like cocking a snook—putting your fingers to your nose. She clutched her . . . em . . . in both hands, turning an awful colour, and glaring as she did so."

"No, miss. She was probably suffering from a spasm. A great many ladies have trouble with their spleen. I remember . . ."

"Never mind her," said Emily quickly, wishing to forget Mrs. Otterley's visit as soon as possible. "I must consult you, Mrs. Middleton, and MacGregor. I am giving an impromptu dinner tomorrow night."

"Certainly," said Rainbird. "I will fetch them now."

Soon Mrs. Middleton, Rainbird, and Angus MacGregor were busily discussing menus. At first MacGregor was quite animated about the whole thing, for he enjoyed every chance to show off his genius as a chef. But when Rainbird and Emily were deciding it would be best if Mrs. Middleton continued in her role of chaperone for the dinner party, Angus fell quiet.

Emily finished her discussion with Rainbird and turned back to the cook. He looked red all over, reflected Emily, bright red hair poking out under his white skull-cap, bright red face . . .

"Angus!" she realised Rainbird was saying in alarm. "Are you all right?"

"I feel verra hot," said Angus, putting a hand to his brow. "It came over me, sudden-like."

"Perhaps you had better go and lie down," said Emily anxiously. "We must have you well for tomorrow."

"Aye," said Angus. He rose to his feet and stood there, swaying.

Rainbird caught him round the waist and supported him to the door. Soon, both men could be heard mounting the stairs.

"Oh, dear," said Mrs. Middleton. "I do hope Angus will not be ill tomorrow. There is his book of recipes and I think I could contrive to cook the dinner myself, Miss Goodenough, but it is not the same. I mean . . . a *she*-cook!"

"Yes," said Emily gloomily. That much she had learned in her servant days. No one who was anyone kept a she-cook.

Upstairs, Rainbird put Angus to bed, promising to bring him up some powders to reduce the fever, which appeared to be increasing its grip on the cook. He then made his way down. On the first landing stood Mr. Goodenough, straightening his cravat in the old mirror that was hung there on the wall.

The glass was very bad and had the effect of making people's reflections look as twisted as poor Mr. Goodenough's face actually was. The butler glanced over Mr. Goodenough's shoulder and stiffened.

For the butler's face in the glass was twisted, but the old mirror had the opposite effect on Mr. Goodenough's features. They were strangely straightened out and he looked as he had before the apoplexy.

And that was how Rainbird remembered where he had seen Mr. Goodenough before.

When Rainbird had been a footman some years ago in Lord Trumpington's household, his master had stopped on the road north at the home of a certain Sir Harry Jackson. Spinks, Sir Harry's butler, had been very kind to the green young footman, John Rainbird. What on earth was Spinks doing masquerading as a gentleman? And who was this niece?

"Is anything the matter, Rainbird?" asked Mr. Goodenough, turning around.

"No, sir," said Rainbird quietly. "Nothing at all."

# Chapter Eight

*Dear to my soul art thou, May Fair!*
*There greatness breathes her native air;*
*There Fashion in her glory sits;*
*Sole spot still unprofaned by Cits.*

*We fix your bounds, ye rich and silly,*
*Along the road by Piccadilly.*

—Anon

What a day!

Emily looked down the dining-table and could not believe she had finally achieved it. The guests were seated and the food was superb.

Apart from herself and Mrs. Middleton and Mr. Goodenough, the earl and Mr. Fitzgerald, there were Lord and Lady Jammers, Lord Agnesby, and two slightly age-ing débutantes, Miss Harriet Giles-Denton and Miss Bessie Plumtree. Lord and Lady Jammers had been kind and easy to talk to when Emily had met them at various social functions, Lord Agnesby, she considered harmless, and Miss Plumtree and Miss Giles-Denton had been selected from the ranks of the débutantes because Emily felt she ought to have *some* young ladies present, and she would not for a minute admit to herself she had chosen them because she privately considered them to be small competition to herself. Miss Giles-Denton was a soft, pale, shapeless blonde, and Miss Plumtree was an angry-looking little brunette whose appearance had grown angrier as each unsuccessful Season came and went.

The day had been hectic. A doctor had had to be summoned for Angus MacGregor. Angus had been bled, which had reduced his fever but had left him as weak as a kitten. He had been carried downstairs and placed on a makeshift bed on the kitchen floor where he had, in a feeble voice, given the frantic staff instructions as to how to prepare the dishes. Mrs. Middleton had discovered a rare talent in herself for the higher arts of cuisine. Although frightened, flustered, and rushed off her feet, the timid housekeeper had never felt so *important* before. Just before the guests arrived, Rainbird sent her upstairs to change her gown and to take her place with the guests as Emily's chaperone.

Emily, regal in a classic Greek gown of white muslin with gold key embroidery, presided at one end of the table and Mr. Goodenough at the other. As the guests ate heartily and cried their praises over the delicacy of the sauces, and Lord Agnesby enquired about the name of the cook and, on learning it, swore that only a man could produce such creations of genius, Emily began to feel for the first time as if she were part of high society. Outside stretched Mayfair, reduced in her mind to the comfortable proportions of an elegant village, a village to which she now belonged. Something had happened to her during that visit from Mrs. Otterley. A great deal of her timidity and fear had left her. She had organised this dinner party—and it was a success. And Emily had indeed joined the ranks of society with that thought, for she had forgotten for the moment that the success was almost entirely due to the staff of Number 67. She had become so used to accepting their advice on all matters great and small, to relying on Mrs. Middleton to tell her what to wear and how to converse, that the awkward shy Emily was a thing of the past, and she took the servants' help for granted.

But that insecurity about the book, although reduced in her mind to a nagging little anxiety, was still there. She had been conversing in generalities to the Earl of Fleetwood for the first few courses, but with the arrival of the Floating Island pudding, Emily said lightly, "Have you, my lord, read a book about some chambermaid that is just published? The author does not dare give his name but simply has himself described on the title page as A Gentleman."

"I have read the book, yes," said the earl. "I assume you have, too. What did you think of it?"

"Very amusing," said Emily, "but highly improbable. I could not quite believe in the wicked servants or think anyone described in the book could be someone I might meet in real life."

"Bravo!" he said. "Very few people seem to understand all the characters are probably fictional in that undistinguished work."

He sensed a tension in Emily ebbing away and wondered what he had said to ease her mind. She was looking like the princess society had believed her to be, he thought. She was beautiful and ladylike. Nor had she dropped one common expression. She was poised and assured and very much the hostess. But he sharply remembered the other

Emily with a certain indefinable something in her eyes like a wary animal. What had brought about the change? Probably it was because she had been very countrified on her arrival in London, he decided. He became aware that she had turned the conversation from the subject of his book and was asking him what he thought of the latest production of *The Magic Flute*.

"Very well in its way," he said. "That is—what I could hear of it."

"Some of the music was so beautiful, it made me cry," said Emily, "but I hardly believe Mozart wrote 'The Roast Beef of Old England.' "

"The producer throws several popular English songs into the opera so that the audience can sing along as well. So it makes an evening at the opera rather like an evening in the Coal Hole."

Emily looked puzzled, so he explained, "The Coal Hole is a tavern in the Strand where they have popular balladeers and other entertainments."

"It would be lovely," said Emily wistfully, "if there were an opera house in London for lovers of music, where people did not go simply because it is fashionable to do so."

The earl affected shock. "You are an original, Miss Goodenough." He turned to Miss Giles-Denton on his other side and said, "Miss Goodenough would have an opera house for music lovers only."

Miss Giles-Denton struck an Attitude. It was of Minerva debating whether to inspire a writer or not. It involved a strained look about the eyes and one finger pointing to the middle of the forehead. The earl waited patiently.

"The ladies should not be interested in music," pronounced Miss Giles-Denton at last. "Clothes are more important . . . and dancing."

"Then why do we not confine our displays of clothes and dancing to Almack's and leave the opera alone?" cried Emily.

"Pon rep," said Lord Agnesby indulgently. "You will have us believe you to be a Blue Stocking, Miss Goodenough."

"There must come a day when intelligence is fashionable," said Emily.

"Not for the ladies," said Lord Agnesby. "We adore the ladies. Die for 'em. Pretty little things." He kissed his cochineal-dyed fingers and waved them in the air. "How could we gentlemen cope with the harsh realities of life were it not for some angel sustaining us with her innocent prattle?"

There was a murmur of agreement from all but the earl, who looked cynically amused. It was rumoured Lord Agnesby would be more inclined to die for a pretty boy than for any woman. Mrs. Middleton gave her nervous cough, a sign that Emily was in danger of making a cake of herself.

Emily looked down mulishly at the remains of her pudding.

"I see you do not agree," said the earl.

"No, I don't," said Emily, but in a low voice meant for his ears alone. "I like wearing pretty gowns and receiving compliments, but I like books and music, and surely there is nothing wrong in that?"

"Nothing at all in the eyes of the ton— that is, if you confine your reading to trivia such as that book we have been discussing."

"Oh, no."

"Do you read romances?"

"No longer. I consider them mischievous books written for ladies and soldier-officers. They make love the main purpose of life and are, I am sure, responsible for rash engagements and unhappy marriages. Chivalry is quite another thing. I am confident that many can imbibe Don Quixote's high-mindedness without catching his insanity."

"You are right, and yet at this moment I confess love appears to me very important."

Emily looked into his eyes and felt her own glance being trapped and held. Her body began to experience all those nasty, low, vulgar unladylike feelings she had felt in dreams.

"And newspapers," she said breathlessly. "I read many of those."

"There are now so many, the number is bewildering," he said in a caressing, husky voice that seemed to be saying something else entirely.

"There is a poem about them all," said Emily with a shaky laugh and wrenching her gaze away from his. "How does it go? Ah, I have it.

Alas! alas! the *World* is ruined quite!
The *Sun* comes out in the evening
And never gives any light.
Poor *Albion* is no more,
The *Evening Star* does not rise,
And the *True Briton* tells nothing but lies.
Should they supress the *British Press*,
There would be no harm done;
There's no hope that the *Times* will mend,

And it would be no matter,
If the *Globe* were at an end."

"A neat epigram," said the earl, "but not nearly long enough. There are at least 250 newspapers in the United Kingdom. Can you imagine a poem about them all?"

Fitz jealously watched the expressions on the couple's faces as they conversed. He could hear what they were saying—they were talking about newspapers—but their eyes appeared to be carrying on a different conversation entirely. It was just like Fleetwood to talk casually and dismissively about Emily, and then steal a march on them all. Fitz had begun to think seriously about his chances of engaging Emily's affections. She was so very beautiful that he did not think he had much hope. But the sight of his friend making love to her in that blatant, indecent way—and that was what Fleetwood *was* doing, even though he was now talking about literary magazines—had aroused a fierce spirit of competition in Fitz's breast. He would have been amazed and disheartened had he known that Emily had taken two hours to recognise him, having not quite heard his name when he was announced, and assumed the new, clean, and paintless

Fitz was another friend the earl had brought along in his place.

Across the table, Harriet Giles-Denton and Bessie Plumtree exchanged sour looks. They wished they had not come. It was miserable to be so outshone by this interloper into society. For they were sure Emily *was* an interloper. No one had ever heard of the Goodenoughs before. There had been some tarradiddle about her being a princess, but that had quickly died away. Jealousy sharpened their perceptions wonderfully. They noticed Emily's speech, although clear and almost accentless, contained none of the French phrases or lisping baby talk currently fashionable among the débutantes. She held very odd views, almost radical. They both suspected Miss Emily Goodenough of being a Jacobite.

As the earl talked to Emily, the rest of the room went away. He was aware only of her. He wondered vaguely who she really was, and almost in the same moment decided it did not matter. Like most aristocrats, he could be extremely single-minded when he had set his heart on something.

By the close of the dinner party, as she stood up with one fluid, graceful movement to lead the ladies downstairs to the front parlour, which had been given the elevated title of drawing-room for that evening, he knew the something he wanted more than anything in the world was Miss Emily Goodenough.

No sooner were the ladies in the drawing-room than Miss Plumtree and Miss Giles-Denton begged Emily to play them something on the spinet in the back parlour. Emily, who had never been taught to play, threw a glance of appeal at Mrs. Middleton.

"*I* shall play for you, ladies," said Mrs. Middleton stoutly. She had not played in years and was distressed to find when she sat down and looked at the music that she could remember the right hand very well— but what did one do with the left?

She fumbled away inexpertly while Emily sat down beside Lady Jammers and plunged into a long description of a play she had seen.

Bessie Plumtree and Harriet Giles-Denton were rapidly coming to the happy conclusion that Emily was quite plain. When one is jealous of some woman, one is not only in competition with her but looking down on her at the same time, which all makes the defect of jealousy almost unrecognisable in oneself. The brightness and largeness of her eyes they put down to an application of belladonna, the trimness of her waist to corsets, and the glory of her hair to a wig.

The gentlemen did not stay very long in the dining-room, but long enough for Bessie and Harriet to have decided Emily was nothing out of the common way. They were, therefore, amazed that the handsome earl should go straight to Emily's side as soon as he entered the room.

Fitz tried to talk to Bessie and Harriet, but his eyes remained fixed on Emily and the earl. What were they saying? Would he have a chance to speak to Emily and persuade her to go driving with him? And what had she just said that had startled Fleetwood so?

Emily had just told the earl of his sister's visit.

"I have no doubt," he said furiously, "that she came to warn you I was a murderer."

"Yes, she did," said Emily.

"And you believed her," he said bitterly. It was a statement, not a question.

"No," said Emily. "I prefer to make up my own mind about people rather than listen to gossip, because that is how I would have people treat me."

"You believe in blind trust?"

"To a certain extent, yes."

"Will you marry me, Miss Goodenough?"

They were standing by the window. Emily clutched the curtain for support.

"My lord, you jest!"

"Not I. I am deadly serious. Will you marry me?"

Emily looked up into his blue eyes, at his handsome face, and longed to say yes.

"I am afraid of marriage," she said, plucking nervously at the curtain. "I fear I am a romantic, and there is nothing romantic in furious sisters, marriage settlements, and lengthy arrangements."

"We will be married by special licence and dispense with all the formalities," he said promptly.

Fitz came up to them just then, but the earl flashed him an angry look and Emily did not look at him at all.

Fitz gloomily walked away and tried to show interest in Bessie and Harriet.

"But the announcement in the newspaper will cause a furor," said Emily.

"Then we will announce our marriage after the wedding."

Emily gave a shaky laugh. "I cannot believe this is happening. You know nothing about me."

"If you are prepared to disbelieve my sister and take me on trust, then I am prepared to believe only the best of you. Marry me!"

"Oh, this is ridiculous . . . you should ask my uncle's permission. And where should we live?"

"Anywhere. I have my home in the country, a shooting-box in Yorkshire, a crumbling castle in Scotland, that house in Grosvenor Square from which I will gladly eject my sister, my rented place in Park Lane, or—"

"Or here," said Emily quietly.

"Here! My dear Miss Emily!"

But it had just dawned on Emily what a support and prop these odd rented servants at Number 67 were. How could she face a new and strange household staff so soon?

He shrugged. "If you wish. But only for a few weeks. I say, does that mean you *will* marry me?"

Emily felt exalted with triumph. She, the ex-chambermaid, would be a countess! In a few weeks, in a few months, the very fact she *was* a countess would stop anyone from questioning her background. And this earl was suggesting they should be married without publicity, notoriety, or fuss.

She took a deep breath.

"Yes," she said.

The guests did not stay very long. Even by the gourmand standards of the beginning of the nineteenth century, all had eaten vast amounts, and, with the exception of the elated earl and the jealous Fitz, were becoming drowsy.

Rainbird stood in the hall to assist the guests into wraps and cloaks, his hand discreetly held out to collect tips. Lord and Lady Jammers were very generous—ten guineas; Bessie and Harriet, anxious to show this upstart they were monied ladies, almost equally so; Fitz gave five guineas because he was always generous; the earl gave twenty because he was walking on air; Lord Agnesby alone ignored Rainbird's outstretched hand.

The earl told Mr. Goodenough he would call on him at noon the following day, and then they all disappeared into the night.

Mrs. Middleton thankfully stopped murdering Haydn and said she must go downstairs and attend to Angus.

"When you have seen to his comfort," said Emily, "I wish all the staff to assemble in the parlour. I have an announcement to make."

"What announcement, Emily?" asked Mr. Goodenough when they were alone.

"Fleetwood is going to marry me!" cried Emily, pirouetting around the room.

Mr. Goodenough sat down suddenly. "We can't. *You* can't," he said in a shaky voice. "His lawyers will soon find us out."

"Not they," said Emily with a laugh and told him all about the earl's odd proposal and the understanding the wedding should be in secret.

Mr. Goodenough clasped his hands to stop their shaking. "But only think, Emily. *After* you are married, after the first flush of romance is over, *then* he will begin to ask questions—who were your parents, where is your home, all that sort of thing."

"He *trusts* me," said Emily stubbornly. "Oh, please be happy for me. And we are to stay *here*, for I need these odd servants to sustain me."

"But this is only a rented house. We cannot rely on Rainbird and Mrs. Middleton forever."

"Oh, be happy for me! Did we not come to London to find me a husband? Have I not found one? Do not lose courage now."

Downstairs, the staff were gleefully counting out the takings. "I thought that skinflint, Lord Agnesby, might have parted with something," mourned Rainbird, "but not even a threepenny bit!"

"But he did!" said Mrs. Middleton. "And not only that, he gave me a note for Mr. MacGregor. He gave me ten guineas and this letter which says . . . Wait a minute, I shall read it to Angus."

She knelt down beside the cook where he lay on his makeshift bed. "Do but listen, Angus," she said. "Lord Agnesby says, 'My dear chef, You are a Genius, and your talents would raise the Dead. Never have I enjoyed such exquisite Fare, Agnesby.' There!"

Angus smiled weakly up at the housekeeper. "You did all the work, Mrs. Middleton," he said. "You are as fine a lady as ever set foot in Mayfair." He reached up a long hairy arm, clasped the startled housekeeper about the waist, drew her down to him, and deposited a smacking kiss on her lips.

The staff all cheered as Mrs. Middleton, flustered and dazed and straightening her cap with shaking fingers, stumbled to her feet.

"Now," said Rainbird, "Miss Emily has an announcement to make and wants us all upstairs. But before we go, there is something I must tell you. Mr. Goodenough is an impostor."

"That dear old man!" cried Lizzie. "Surely not."

"He has suffered some sort of apoplexy which has twisted his face," said Rainbird, "but I recently remembered where I had seen him before. His name was Spinks and he was butler to a certain Mr. Harry Jackson up in the north."

"And Miss Emily?"

"I fear she is an adventuress."

There was a stunned silence.

Then, "I don't care," said Mrs. Middleton. "She is a dear, sweet lady, and I am sure she has never done anything wrong."

"We'll talk about it later," said Rainbird. "But I think we all must decide to be loyal to both of them. What they were before does not concern us."

There was a murmur of agreement.

But their loyalty was badly shaken when Emily proudly made her announcement. If Emily was an adventuress, then she was

151

flying too high. If she introduced common blood into the earl's family through pretending to be someone else and was found out, she might go to prison—after the marriage was annulled.

Still, they all put a brave face on it and wished her well.

Emily began to tease the ladies about their marriage prospects, while Rainbird studied her radiant face and wondered if she had considered the fact that the days of the Mayfair Chapel where one could be married for a guinea and no questions asked were long past. She would need to produce papers proving she was who she said she was. As the servants began to joke and relax, he slipped from the room and went quietly up the stairs.

He went straight to the desk in Emily's bedroom. It was locked. He fished in his pocket for his bunch of keys and searched through them until he found the tiny spare key to the desk. Quietly he opened it and, carrying a branch of candles over to the desk, he sat down and began to read through a small pile of papers. And there, finally, was the registration paper of Emily's birth from the parish of Burton Hampton in Cumberland. Born, Emily Jenkins; mother,

Rachel Pretty, housemaid; father, Ebeneezer Jenkins, blacksmith. There were also papers to prove she had changed her name legally and then a copy of Sir Harry Jackson's will in which he had left everything to his butler, Spinks. So their only crime was pretending to be a gentleman and lady. Any money they had legally belonged to Spinks, now legally Benjamin Goodenough. Rainbird replaced all the papers. He was about to lock the desk when he changed his mind and extracted the parish registration of Emily's birth. He slipped it into his pocket and made his way downstairs in time for a final glass of champagne.

Later that evening, when Mrs. Middleton was about to prepare for bed, she thought about Angus MacGregor. His fever appeared to have abated. The doctor had said it had probably been caused by an inflammation of the lungs.

Mrs. Middleton hesitated, trembling, and then she stiffened her spine, picked up a book in one hand and a candle in the other, and made her way up to the attic where Angus slept. Rainbird and Joseph were still downstairs in the servants' hall, and so the cook was alone. Joseph and Rainbird had helped him upstairs to his bed as soon as Emily's party was over.

Mrs. Middleton set the candle down beside the bed and said softly, "Are you awake, Mr. MacGregor?"

"Aye," said the cook. "Thon was a grand letter from Agnesby. It got me fair excited. What brings you here, Mrs. Middleton?"

"I thought it might settle you for the night if I read to you."

"That would be fine."

And so Mrs. Middleton began.

"The stag at eve had drunk his fill,
Where danced the moon on Monan's rill,
And deep, his midnight lair had made
In lone Glenartney's hazel shade."

The words of Walter Scott's *Lady of the Lake* fell gently on the cook's ear. His hand crept out from beneath the covers and he took hold of the housekeeper's mittened hand. She started and blushed but let him retain her hand and went on reading until Rainbird and Joseph crept in. Joseph looked at the unlikely couple's joined hands and opened his mouth to say something, but Rainbird nudged him hard and glared him into silence.

# Chapter Nine

*It is in truth a most contagious game;*
HIDING THE SKELETON, shall be its name.
— George Meredith

Emily hardly slept, torn between fear and elation. Ambition had driven any amorous thoughts she might have held for the Earl of Fleetwood straight out of her pretty head.

Somehow, everything would be manageable after they were married. For the first few weeks, she would have the servants to support her. As a timid girl will inflict her mother on her new husband's household, so Emily was prepared to inflict the rented house and its rented servants on the earl. She did not consider the earl's thoughts and dreams. That a high-born earl might have fears and worries of his own never entered Emily's mind. She naïvely supposed a title protected any human from the insecurities and uncertainties that plagued common mortals like herself.

She rose and dressed with great care in an

elaborate morning gown. It was of white muslin with a high ruffled collar and three deep lace flounces at the hem. The sleeves were long and tight and ended in points at her wrist. She dressed her hair à *la angélique* and then decided the centre parting made her look too severe. Her hair had a natural curl, but Emily heated the curling tongs and tried to make it curlier. Curls fell over her eyes and down her back but would not allow themselves to be twisted into any fashionable coiffure. Her arms began to ache with the effort of trying to arrange her hair and a sudden fit of nerves made her drop the brush with a clatter onto the floor.

She heard voices from the street below and crossed to the window and looked down.

Lizzie, the scullery maid, was leaning on a sweeping brush and talking to a tall footman. Emily recognised the footman as being the one from next door.

He looked very handsome and Lizzie looked young and pretty and carefree.

Emily's heart gave a lurch. What if she had stayed in her position as servant? Perhaps she, too, might be standing there receiving the flattering attentions of some footman. In that moment, Emily envied Lizzie from the bottom of her heart.

As if aware of her gaze, Lizzie looked up, said something to Luke, who smiled and walked away, and then she began sweeping the pavement outside the house.

It must be wonderful, thought Lizzie, to be a lady like Miss Emily—and she *is* a lady; I don't care what Mr. Rainbird says—and be able to have a handsome man fall in love with you and be able to get married, just like that.

Lizzie had promised at last to go out walking with Luke. She did not like Luke, but she was very flattered by his attentions. Too many times had Joseph snubbed poor Lizzie because she was only a scullery maid. It would be wonderful to show Joseph she could attract a first footman, who was a cut above a mere rented ordinary footman such as Joseph in the servants' pecking order. The servants had been discussing their pub that morning at breakfast, and once more it had seemed to Lizzie that all that was expected of her was that she should continue to work in the kitchen. But it also seemed expected, though nothing definite had been said, that, of course, she would marry Joseph. Now that idea would have sent Lizzie into seventh heaven only a short time ago. But Lizzie's head had been turned by Luke's attention and she was beginning to feel she was worthy of someone *better* than Joseph. The dream about Joseph marching home in the evening from the fields had been vastly silly. Joseph would never do anything that might soil his white hands. He even wore gloves when he cleaned the silver, and he often sat in the evenings polishing and manicuring his nails, as fastidious as the kitchen cat.

Lizzie's thoughts turned once more to Luke. He *was* very handsome, and he always told her she looked pretty. That Luke had proved in the past to have a spiteful streak was forgotten by Lizzie. She would be the only scullery maid in London who had attracted the attention of a first footman. First footmen certainly were not known to stoop so low.

Luke had said she was to ask Rainbird for permission to walk out with him that evening for an hour. Lizzie knew the butler did not like Luke, but she also knew he would give her permission if only to annoy Joseph.

The same ambition that fired Emily also fired Lizzie. She gave the pavement a last angry sweep with her broom and then choked. A little pile of dust had been left by the dust-cart and it swirled up about her, covering her dress in fine white ash and soiling her shoes.

Lizzie sighed and went downstairs to clean herself.

"Seen a ghost?" jeered Joseph. "You're all white."

Lizzie compressed her lips and threw him an angry look before making her way to the scullery pump. "It's Friday," called Joseph after her.

No water was pumped up to London houses on a Friday. Lizzie slammed the door of the scullery and began to take off her soiled gown. She would use one of the pails of water that had been drawn the day before for dish-washing.

Above her head, she heard the rumble of an arriving carriage and Rainbird's exclamation of "Noon already! That'll be his lordship. That scrivener had better be here in a minute or I'll murder him."

Upstairs, the Earl of Fleetwood was soon closeted with Mr. Goodenough in the front parlour. Rainbird served wine. He took up a position inside the door instead of leaving the room.

Mr. Goodenough looked ill and miserable.

"You know why I am come?" asked the earl.

"Yes, my lord," said Mr. Goodenough gloomily.

"And I have your permission?"

"Yes, my lord."

"You are perhaps unhappy because of the rush and secrecy of this proposed marriage. I am prepared to be married with full pomp and ceremony in several months' time, if that would please you better."

"*No!*" squeaked Mr. Goodenough.

"Now as to the matter of dowry and marriage settlements . . ."

"I am not well, my lord, not well *at all!*" exclaimed Mr. Goodenough, tugging at his cravat. "I have no head for business."

"Then our lawyers . . ."

"I *hate* lawyers."

Rainbird crossed to the window and looked out as if searching for someone.

Emily entered the room. The earl stood up and bowed before her.

She looked anxiously at her distressed "uncle" and then at the earl. "Have you not received my uncle's permission?" she asked.

"I have Mr. Goodenough's permission," said the earl, "but I am afraid I have distressed him with business matters."

"But I thought we were going to dispense with such mundane and unromantic arrangements," cried Emily.

The earl hesitated. It went against tradition, it went against the grain, *not* to discuss financial arrangements. But she was so very beautiful and she had trusted *him*. The least he could do was to repay that trust.

"Very well," he said. "I shall arrange a special licence today. But you must observe some formalities."

Rainbird gave an exclamation and darted from the room.

"Such as?" asked Emily, striving to appear calm.

"I must have your papers—the parish registration of your birth."

"I would like to sit down," said Emily in a small voice. She knew now she would have to refuse him. He would see that paper and then demand to know why she had changed her name. He would know her parents had been common folk. Perhaps, in his fury, he would denounce her to society.

The earl waited patiently as she sat down, and still more patiently as she looked down at her hands, frozen in silence.

"The papers, Miss Goodenough," he prompted gently.

161

"Ah, yes, the papers," said Emily wildly. "Uncle, pray leave us. There is something I wish to say to Lord Fleetwood."

Mr. Goodenough walked over to Emily, bent down, and kissed her cheek. "I am so sorry," he whispered.

The earl's heart sank. There was something awfully wrong in his asking for her papers. She wished to conceal the secret of her birth. And if that secret was so terrible, then he had better *not* marry her. He could always take her to Gretna Green in Scotland and marry her without any identification, but he felt in his bones she would not want to do that, to prolong the masquerade—if she was, as he suspected again, acting a part.

Rainbird appeared again and crossed the room to Emily's side. "Your papers, ma'am," he said.

Emily turned very pale. "Thank you, Rainbird," she said quietly. "I shall speak to you later. I did not give you permission to search my desk."

She sat looking down at the yellowing piece of paper in her hand. She would hand it to the earl and then the charade would be over.

Then the spidery writing leapt from the

page. She looked and looked again. Her eyes must be deceiving her. It must be a trick of the light. She carried the paper over to the window and read it with a fast-beating heart. Born 1791, Emily Goodenough. Mother, Rachel Parsons, spinster. Father, Ebeneezer Goodenough, Gentleman.

A faint tinge of colour appeared in her pale cheeks. She could marry the earl after all! Rainbird had found out her secret and had not betrayed her! Somehow he had contrived to forge this document.

But as she looked at the handsome earl, her heart misgave her. How could she deceive him so? How could she go on living a lie? And then ambition took her firmly by the shoulders and pushed her forward. "I think this is what you require, my lord," she said. He thanked her and put the paper in his pocket without looking at it.

"Where is your chaperone, Mrs. Middleton?" he asked. "She has not yet wished me well."

Relieved to be able to confess some truth, Emily said, "Mrs. Middleton is in the servants' hall. She is the housekeeper here. I had to use her services as chaperone for I have no living female relatives and did not know any genteel female when I arrived in London."

"What resourceful servants you seem to have, my love. But we will be married, and very soon, and you need only rely on me."

He walked forward and took her in his arms.

He bent his head and kissed her, a formal chaste kiss on the lips. But Emily had forgotten that real ladies do not have passions. The cool touch of his lips started a fire burning in her own. In the most natural way in the world, she flung her arms around him and kissed him back.

And then he kissed her properly, and Emily moaned in her throat in a most vulgar way and responded with every fibre of her body.

He was deliriously kissing her ears, her neck, her throat, and her lips again when a chill little voice of propriety told him the door was standing open and any gossiping servant who walked across the hall might have an interesting view.

He raised his head and gave her a little shake. "Wait until we are married, my sweet," he said caressingly. "Then we will have all the time in the world for kisses."

Emily blushed miserably. She knew she

had behaved disgracefully. Was not this sort of behaviour just the way that wretched fictional maid, Emilia, had betrayed herself?

But when he bowed and walked to the door, stopped, turned back, and pulled her into his arms again and kissed her feverishly and passionately, Emily's treacherous, wanton, common body betrayed her again, so that when he finally released her and took his leave, she had to stagger to a chair and sit down. It was some time before she could bring herself to summon Rainbird.

When the butler entered the room, Emily said curtly, "Sit down, Rainbird."

"Thank you, ma'am." Rainbird sat primly on the edge of the chair opposite her.

"I am surprised you do not address me as Emily—now that you know we are of the same class," said Emily.

Rainbird gave an infinitesimal shrug. "It is not my duty to question the machinations of my employers," he said.

"You had a registration paper forged," said Emily. "It was very wicked of you—very wicked of you, too, to read my papers. But I thank you from the bottom of my heart. You will not tell anyone?"

"No, Miss Emily."

"Then I am to be the Countess of Fleetwood."

"My felicitations. But, miss, have you not thought it might be wise to tell my lord the truth? He will find out sooner or later."

"Why?" demanded Emily fiercely. "Do I not look like a lady?"

"You *are* a lady," said Rainbird. "But my lord is very much in love with you, and men in love become jealous and suspicious and can *sense* secrets in a woman."

"They say that love is blind," said Emily lightly.

"Only for a little while," said the butler earnestly. "I am sure if my lord knew the truth, he would still marry you."

"He might forgive me for being of common stock," said Emily. "But he would never forgive me for having been a servant. I was a servant in Sir Harry's household. Fleetwood despises servants."

"As to that, it is perhaps because there was a great deal of gossip about his late wife's death."

"Then he should blame his horrible sister for that scandal and not his servants. She called to tell me he had killed his wife!"

"But you did not believe her?"

"Not I. I believe in trusting people."

"But Lord Fleetwood may come to believe *you* did not trust *him* enough. I will tell you why I examined your papers. I recognised Mr. Goodenough as being the former butler, Spinks. Although his face is greatly changed, someone else might recognise him . . . might recognise *you*, Miss Emily."

"I was only in service a short time before Sir Harry's death," said Emily. "I was very young, only sixteen during the last year he was well enough to entertain guests. I have not seen anyone in London society who ever visited Sir Harry. And who ever notices a servant?"

"If you were as pretty then as you are now," said Rainbird cautiously, "some gentleman may well remember you."

"There was one . . . No I refuse to worry about it." Excitement and elation flooded Emily again. "Only think! I am to be a countess."

"Surely my lord means more to you than just a title?" said Rainbird.

"Oh, yes, of course. He is so very handsome—and I will be the envy of so many," added Emily naïvely.

"Do you not think it wise to give matters a little longer, Miss Emily?"

"No," said Emily. "Time may go against me. I mean to be a countess. Now I must go and tell Mr. Goodenough that, thanks to you, all is well."

Rainbird felt a qualm of unease as he went down the stairs to the servants' hall. He felt he had, perhaps, done Emily a disservice by supplying her with forged papers.

Lizzie tugged at his sleeve as he entered and whispered to him she had something to ask him. Joseph was glaring at her suspiciously, so Rainbird led her through to the kitchen, which was empty, for Angus was still in bed recovering from his fever.

"What is it, Lizzie?"

"It's Luke," said Lizzie. "He wants me to get an hour off this evening to go out walking with him."

"It's all right, Lizzie," said Rainbird soothingly. "I'll tell the young whippersnapper to leave you alone."

"Oh, no, Mr. Rainbird. I *want* to go out with him!"

"Lizzie, he is not a very pleasant individual."

"I'm not going to *marry* him," said Lizzie crossly. "Luke is a *first footman*. I shall be the envy of all the girls. He didn't ask Alice or Jenny, he asked *me*."

"You are a pretty little thing, Lizzie, but be careful! He may just be asking you out to spite Joseph."

"I want to go," said Lizzie stubbornly. "He is a first footman and Joseph is only a rented footman."

"You and Miss Emily are much alike," said Rainbird. "Two such pleasant women and both being tricked by vanity."

"That's not nice," said Lizzie hotly. "I never have any fun. Why shouldn't I be allowed to go out?"

"Very well, Lizzie. But only one hour. If you are not back, then we shall all go out looking for you."

Rainbird returned to the servants' hall.

"What was thet whispering all abaht?" asked Joseph languidly.

"Never mind," said Rainbird. "Sometimes I could *shake* you, Joseph. If you were more of a man. . . . Take some more coal up to the parlour and stop lounging about. There's work to be done."

"So you are to be married," said Fitz later that day. "And just like that! I feel you might have warned me your intentions were serious. I was on the point of trying for Miss Goodenough myself."

"I thought you might have guessed when I went out of my way to arrange that rout and set you up as a princess."

"But what of all those doubts of yours about her background?"

"I decided to trust her—but there was no need. Her papers prove her to be of gentle birth."

"Then why all the secrecy about the marriage?"

"Because my beloved wishes it that way. And I do not want my sister's Friday-face to spoil my wedding. Come, wish me well, Fitz. You will make an excellent bride-man."

"I wish you all the best in the world with my better feelings. My nastier feelings, nonetheless, tell me that you deliberately tried to persuade me Miss Emily was common to put me out of the running."

"My dear Fitz, you never even reached the starting-gate until that dinner party of hers!"

"True," said Fitz with a reluctant grin. "Ah, well, perhaps there will be another beauty to take my eye. I am feeling out of sorts. I have not yet grown into my new appearance and I confess I feel a dull dog in these sober clothes."

"You can peacock as much as you like on my wedding-day."

"So we shall be losing you," said Fitz. "Where are you spending your honeymoon?"

"At Sixty-seven Clarges Street."

"Bedad! Why?"

"My love is attached to her rented servants. That Mrs. Middleton is none other than the housekeeper."

"I thought that *you* would not countenance an affection for mere servants."

"If I can have my Emily, I can put up with anything. The house has proved lucky for me. Besides, I shall only have to endure the place for a few weeks."

With her hair dressed up on top of her head, quite like a lady, and wearing a warm brown shawl over her green-and-white-striped gown, Lizzie stepped out proudly that evening on Luke's arm.

She barely heard what he was saying, but he was bragging about himself, and Lizzie, who had become used to just such monologues from Joseph, felt free to bask in all the glory of walking along beside this splendid young man.

She saw Mary, the housemaid at Number

171

62, staring open-mouthed, and Lizzie felt her heart would burst with joy.

It was early evening and a green and violet sky stretched out over the tops of the jumbled chimneys of Buckingham House as they walked down through the Green Park. Trees with their new buds stood silhouetted in the twilight like black lace and blackbirds carolled their spring song out on the quiet, sleepy, smoky London air.

"Must be hard to be a scullery maid," Lizzie realised Luke was saying. "You being eddicated and all."

"Oh, I don't mind," said Lizzie, who felt nothing could worry her on this lovely evening.

"Still, you're a pretty little girl, and it must go hard not having a dowry."

"Oh, I got a dowry," said Lizzie. "Well, it's my share of the pub."

"Pub? What pub?"

Lizzie felt she should not tell Luke about their plans. But the desire to show off was stronger. She tossed her head.

"We've been saving up ever so hard. We got nigh on three hundred pounds among us."

Luke whistled softly. "That's enough to

buy a pub already. Wot you all waiting for?"

"Mr. Rainbird says as how we must have more for the stocks, the glasses, the linen, and enough laid aside to keep us till we get a trade."

Luke slid an arm about Lizzie's slender waist. "That Rainbird's a stupid fellow. He could make ten times as much by the end o' next week if he used his brain-box."

"Go on," giggled Lizzie. She made to pull away, but then she saw one of the grooms from Lambeth Mews at the end of Clarges Street, who was cutting through the park staring at them, and stayed where she was.

"It's the truth. Lord Hampshire's got a filly running at Ascot at ten to one, and I 'appen to know the other 'orses, horses, has been nobbled. Now, say you took that money and gave it to me to put on, you'd be able to give 'em three thousand pounds. Think o' the looks on their faces! Three fousand—thousand! Why, none of you'd need to work in a pub. You could invest that on Change and live on the proceeds."

"I'd never do that," said Lizzie, pulling away this time. " 'Member when Joseph took the money and put it all on a horse and lost it all?"

"Joseph. That milksop!"

"Thought he was a friend of yours. Anyway, he's a friend of mine, and I don't like you calling him names!"

"He's a friend o' mine, too, Lizzie, but come now, you must confess he ain't got much brain. This filly's going to win 'cos I got it from Hampshire's valet."

"How much you putting on?"

"Five shillings. Don't laugh. It's all I got."

"They'd never let me have the money," said Lizzie. "They'd laugh at me."

"Well, don't tell them! Think o' their faces when you comes in and throws the money on the table."

It was a lovely dream, but Lizzie shook her head.

"You see, Lizzie," said Luke earnestly, "the reason I'm asking is this. I've taken a fancy to you, so help me, I have. Your share o' the winnings would give you enough for us to be married and set up a business on our own. I know, we'd buy a little cottage in the country, a little bit of land, and you'd keep house and I'd work the land."

He slid a coaxing arm about her waist. Lizzie closed her eyes and leaned against him. It was so like that dream she had had of herself and Joseph. But Luke was not Joseph. He was tall and strong and extremely masculine. She saw a pretty little cottage, a garden full of flowers, and now it was Luke who marched towards her down the country road, and not Joseph.

"I couldn't do it," she whispered. "It would be stealing."

Luke turned her face up to his and kissed her gently on the mouth. A passionate kiss would have frightened Lizzie, but Luke's soft kiss was warm and reassuring. "I am being proposed to by a *first footman*," thought Lizzie dizzily.

Then she remembered the days when Luke had been courting Alice, and how Luke had once twisted her arm so hard he had bruised it.

"You was after Alice once," said Lizzie, drawing away.

"Alice ain't the kind you *marry*," said Luke with a scornful laugh. "Listen, let me tell you about that cottage where we'll live. . . ."

He began to talk long and earnestly, interrupting his speech from time to time to kiss Lizzie and to stroke her hair. Dazed, flattered, happy, elated, and made thoroughly vain for the first time in her life, Lizzie listened to him, and the more he talked and the more he kissed and caressed, the more Lizzie hardened her heart against her "family"—the other servants. They had let her sleep on a damp pallet on the scullery floor, and her situation had only improved after she had fallen ill and one of the tenants had insisted she have a proper bed to sleep in. When they had nearly all been arrested for stealing one of the King's deer and she had saved them by slashing her own wrist so that the blood on the area steps was believed to have been hers and not that of the stolen deer, they had not done one thing to make her lot in life any better. Yes, they had been kind when she was recovering, but after that, they had piled the menial jobs on her much as they had done before.

The sky was growing dark. By the time Rainbird's voice could be heard, shouting, "Lizzie! Lizzie!" she and Luke had become conspirators.

Mr. Percival Pardon was back in London after a long absence. He was low on funds and could not entertain as lavishly as he would have liked, but he had invited his old friends, Mrs. Plumtree and Mrs. Giles-Denton and their daughters, Bessie and Harriet, to tea. He drank in all the gossip like a thirsty man who had been deprived of water for a long time.

"And so," said Mrs. Giles-Denton after a long bout of highly satisfactory scandal, "we have had quite a busy time. I forgot to tell you, we were persuaded to let the dear girls go to that wretched house in Clarges Street."

"Oh yes?" said Mr. Pardon, that wretched house holding bad memories for him, for his efforts to ruin one of the previous tenants had brought him nothing but disgrace.

"Yes, and I wish I had gone with them. For the tenant is a most odd female no one has ever heard of—a Miss Emily Good-enough."

"And is she pretty?"

"Nothing out of the common way," said Bessie. "Fleetwood was monstrous taken with the creature. But I think she is vulgar. Didn't you think she was *vulgaire*, Harriet?"

Harriet reluctantly gave up her latest Attitude, which was of Pallas Athene looking down from Mount Olympus on Troy. It was an uncomfortable Attitude since it involved standing on one foot with the other foot raised behind and the hand shading the eyes while one arm clutched an imaginary shield.

"Oh, yes, quite *dégoûtant* how all the men fluttered around her."

"A new beauty," mused Mr. Pardon, correctly interpreting all this spite. "Must have a look at her."

# Chapter Ten

*His lordship may compel us to be equal upstairs, but there will never be equality in the servants' hall.*

—Sir James Barrie

The rigid hierarchy of the servants' hall was not observed in winter. And during the Season, it was usually less strict than in most households in the West End of London. But the flurry and work and rushing about caused by Emily's wedding kept the servants firmly in their appointed places. Only by working like a well-drilled regiment with Rainbird as their colonel could they cope with the work and preparations. And down at the bottom of the servants' social ladder was Lizzie. No one had time to pay her any special marked attention. Angus, recovered from his sick-bed and wrestling over preparations for the wedding breakfast, rapped out orders to Lizzie, experimented with sauces, decided against them, and gave her the resultant sticky mess to scrub. Dave, the pot boy, was being used to run errands.

And so Luke's proposal and plans for their marriage sang in Lizzie's tired brain. She forgot all the many kindnesses of the other servants, forgot she was allowed to study, to take walks, to wear pretty gowns, all favours not allowed to less fortunate scullery maids, and, for the first time in her life, grew tight-lipped and surly.

Joseph alone noticed the change in her, but tried to jeer and tease her out of it instead of simply asking her what had come over her.

Lizzie knew where their money was hidden. Palmer had once stolen it, and since that awful day, their savings had reposed in a tin box buried in the ground under a loose paving stone out in the yard. The day before Emily's wedding was to be the day Lord Hampshire's horse ran at Ascot. Lizzie had not been to church for some time. She forgot that gaining a position in a West End household had once seemed like the realisation of a dream.

She became more tired and more irritable but would still have never dreamt of touching their money had she not fallen into disgrace two days before the wedding.

Angus came back into the scullery carrying a copper saucepan and set it down beside Lizzie with a thump. "D'ye call this clean?" demanded the cook. "There's still stuff sticking to the bottom of it."

"*I'm tired* of scrubbing pot after pot," said Lizzie. "Leave it for Dave."

"It's *your* job, girl," said Angus curtly. "Scrub out that pot immediately."

"There was no need for this pot to be scrubbed in the first place," snapped Lizzie. "You and your sauces! Trying one and then the other. You do it deliberately just so's to give me more work!"

"Don't be daft," said the cook, "and don't put on those hoity-toity airs wi' me."

"Why don't you scrub the bloody thing yourself?" screamed Lizzie, her nerve snapping.

Her voice carried clear through into the servants' hall. Rainbird came striding into the scullery, demanding to know what the matter was.

"This idiot of a girl is refusing to scrub the pots and she *swore* at me," said Angus.

"What did she say?"

"She said 'bloody,'" said Angus.

Overworked and rushed off his feet, Rainbird forgot that Lizzie was a friend as well as a scullery maid. Without pausing for thought, he dealt with Lizzie as any other butler would have dealt with a foul-mouthed kitchen maid. He grabbed her by the hair, twisted her head under his arm, seized a bar of yellow soap, and polished her mouth with it.

"That will be enough from you, miss," he said. "Get on with your work."

Without a word, Lizzie bent over the sink. Rainbird hesitated in the doorway of the scullery. Lizzie's thin shoulders were shaking with sobs.

He shook his head in exasperation and walked out.

That night, after all the servants had fallen asleep, Lizzie, white and tense, went out into the yard and lifted the box with their savings up out of the ground, replaced the paving stone, and went to bed with the box tucked under the end of her blankets.

She had had a hurried consultation with Luke at the top of the area steps earlier in the day and had promised to hand him the box if he could contrive to be outside Number 67 at six in the morning.

On the day of her wedding, Emily was feeling dazed and frightened. She had gone through a wedding rehearsal the day before with the earl in a dark and undistinguished church called St. Stephen's in one of the back wynds of the City of London.

Her wedding day dawned dark and rainy —a bad omen.

Alice, Jenny, and Mrs. Middleton arrived in her bedchamber at nine in the morning to array her in her wedding gown. It was not a traditional wedding gown, none of them wanting to alert the gossipy dressmakers of London. It was of white Brussels lace, made more like a morning gown than anything else, and on her head, instead of a veil, she wore a coronet of white silk roses and pearls.

Emily reflected she had not had a chance to talk to her future husband since his proposal. He had even left her immediately after the wedding rehearsal, saying he had some last-minute business to attend to.

Mr. Fitzgerald was to be bride-man and Mrs. Middleton was to be bridesmaid. It was all so wrong, thought Emily wretchedly. She was getting married under false pretences. The marriage would stand, no matter what happened, for Emily Goodenough was, by law, her real name. But, oh, how pleasant it would be to be married openly with all the earl's relatives present, even his obnoxious sister, instead of rushing off to some dark church in this hole-and-corner way.

"But I am to be a countess," Emily reminded herself fiercely, "and nothing else matters."

When Emily was dressed, Mrs. Middleton made a little shooing motion with her hands and Jenny and Alice left the room.

Mrs. Middleton drew up a chair and sat down beside Emily. She was wearing the purple gown and turban she had worn when she was pretending to be the "princess's" lady-in-waiting.

"My dear Miss Emily," she said gently. "I wish I were related to you and then I would know how to counsel you as a young lady should be counselled on her wedding day."

"Do not worry, Mrs. Middleton," said Emily. "I have a good memory and will not make mistakes during the service."

"Ahem." Mrs. Middleton dabbed at her mouth with a silk lace-edged handkerchief and turned a severe look on the curtains. "I am talking about the . . . hem . . . delicate side of marriage."

"Oh." Emily blushed. It all rushed on

her at once. She had only thought of being a countess; she had thought no farther than that.

"What is expected of me?" she asked in a whisper.

Mrs. Middleton had searched her memory for suitable advice during the night. She had been bridesmaid a long, long time ago and had overheard the mother advising the bride, and so she decided the best thing she could do was to pass that advice on to Emily.

"You will share a bed with his lordship tonight, Miss Emily."

"Yes."

"You must remember at all times to love and respect your husband, no matter what happens. Men have strange ways."

"Go on," said Emily. "What do I do?"

"You close your eyes very tightly and think of the king."

Emily blinked. "King George?"

"Yes. His Majesty."

"But I do not see how thinking of a mad king will take my mind off things."

Mrs. Middleton was deeply shocked. "You must not utter such seditious words. His Majesty is unwell, that is all. He is a fine and noble gentleman."

185

"But should I not be thinking of my husband?"

"The intimate acts of marriage are difficult for us ladies," said Mrs. Middleton, and Emily, not knowing the "Mrs." was only a courtesy title, thought the housekeeper was speaking from experience. "Only very low women share the lusts and passions of men."

"Like me," thought Emily bleakly, although she did not voice that thought aloud.

"But everything will be all right," said Mrs. Middleton comfortingly. "I have never yet known a lady die from the experience." She patted Emily's hand. "Now I have put your mind at rest, I must go downstairs and make sure everything is ready for the wedding breakfast."

After she had left, Emily buried her head in her hands. How could she stop herself from responding violently to her husband's kisses and caresses?

"I will think of the king," thought Emily fiercely. "I *will* think of the king.

There was a gentle tap on the door. Emily called "Enter" in a shaky voice. Mr. Goodenough came into the room.

"You look very beautiful, Emily," he said.

"Thank you," muttered Emily, still worrying about the possible reactions of her common body.

"Fleetwood is a fine man," said Mr. Goodenough. "I took the liberty of calling on him to speak to him in private late last night."

"You did not tell him the truth!" exclaimed Emily.

"No," said Mr. Goodenough sadly. "But I was close to it. He is an honourable man and I was sorely tempted to unburden myself, but I did not."

"Then why did you call on him?"

"I feel you would have a better start in marriage were I not present in this house. No! Hear me out. You overrode me in the matter of staying here. I know you wish the support of these servants. But they are only rented servants, and soon you must take up your position in his home as his countess. I discussed the matter with him and he agreed that I should move this day to Park Lane. I will be near enough to you without intruding on your marriage."

"Oh, Benjamin," cried Emily, calling him by his first name as she used to do when they walked in the grounds of Sir Harry Jackson's estate. "I cannot face this marriage without you."

"That is not the remark of a woman in love. You *are* in love with him, are you not?"

Emily wanted to cry out that she did not know, that she was in love with the idea of having a title, that she had possibly made a terrible mistake. What had she thought marriage would be like? She had vaguely imagined the earl spending time in his club or in the country while she continued to live with Mr. Goodenough in much the way she had been doing. But Mr. Goodenough looked so frail, so anxious, she had not the heart to burden him with her fears.

"Yes, I am in love with Fleetwood," she said bleakly. "Very."

"Then that's all right," he said, kissing her cheek. "Now, it is almost time to leave."

The next few hours passed like a dream. There was the journey through the rain to the church, there was the earl at the altar, there was his side of the church with quite a few guests—guests he obviously trusted to keep quiet about it—and, on her side, only the servants from Number 67. Goodness! That girl Lizzie looked about to faint. That one sharp image penetrated Emily's dazed thoughts and then everything became dream-like again as she walked up the aisle on Mr. Goodenough's arm.

She felt as if someone else were making the vows for her. The earl looked very grand and remote. The church was dark and cold and a rising wind outside sent thin, dreary shivers of sound down from the bells in the steeple.

Behind the altar were the Ten Commandments picked out in gold; all the thou-shalt-nots to remind the weary sinner of multiple transgressions. The smell of incense mixed with the smell of musk from the guests and with the throat-catching aroma of dry rot from the old building.

And then it was all over. The register was signed and Emily walked out into the rain, no longer Emily Jenkins or Emily Goodenough, but the Countess of Fleetwood.

"Well, here we are, man and wife," said the earl cheerfully as they drove off.

"Yes," said Emily in a small voice.

She looked pale and agitated, but the earl put that down to bride nerves and decided to remain silent for the rest of the journey to allow her to compose herself. But that very silence made Emily feel worse. What was he thinking? Was he already regretting taking such a step? His high-nosed face looked thoughtful and somewhat stern. What did she know of him? His sister had charged him with killing his wife. What if it were true?

At the wedding breakfast, Emily was introduced to some of the earl's relatives— but not his sister, who had not been sent an invitation—and a few friends. She smiled and curtsied to each and then promptly forgot their names.

Round about her came murmurs of appreciation as one after another of Angus' miraculous dishes appeared on the table. Emily began to drink steadily until the room, the dishes, her husband, and the guests became a comfortable blur.

At one point during the meal, the house was rent with a terrible scream which died away in a long, sobbing wail of anguish. Rainbird ran from the room and returned some ten minutes later, his face hard and set. He murmured apologies. One of the kitchen maids had scalded herself, he said. The earl noticed, however, that Rainbird then bent over Mrs. Middleton, who was seated at the table, and murmured something in her ear, and the housekeeper stifled an exclamation of distress.

Emily had drunk too much to be aware of what was going on around her, but the earl saw that Rainbird, Joseph, and the two maids, Alice and Jenny, were looking distressed.

After four hours of eating and drinking, the wedding breakfast came to an end.

The guests made their farewells and went out into the windy, rainy street.

The earl smiled at Emily. "Shall we retire," he said, "and allow the servants to clear the debris?"

"Where to?" asked Emily groggily.

"To our bedchamber."

Emily squinted at the clock and managed to bring it into focus with some difficulty. "It is only five o' clock, Fleetwood," she exclaimed.

"So it is," he agreed amiably. "Come along."

Like an aristocrat to the guillotine, Emily followed him through to their bedchamber, which was in the room behind the dining-room on the first floor.

"Now, my love . . ." began the earl.

From downstairs came screaming and yelling and cursing.

"This is too much on our wedding day,"

said the earl irritably. "Am I always to be plagued by badly behaved servants?"

He rang the bell. Emily sat down and looked dizzily out of the window.

After some time Rainbird answered the bell's summons.

"What," demanded the earl icily, "is the meaning of all the hullabaloo?"

"It is a domestic matter, my lord," said Rainbird stiffly. "My apologies to my lord and my lady."

"Of course it is a domestic matter, since you are all domestics," said the earl testily.

"Ish that girl, Lizzie," said Emily drunkenly. "Looked white in the church. Mush see Lizzie."

"Stay where you are," ordered the earl, realising for the first time just how very drunk his wife was.

"Now, Rainbird . . ."

"We had been saving to buy a public house," said Rainbird evenly. "Although we could not afford a hostelry in London, we could, we estimated, after another Season, have accumulated enough to buy a place in, say, Highgate. Lizzie, the scullery maid, was duped by Luke, Lord Charteris' first footman, into handing over our savings. Luke said that Lord Hampshire's horse, at ten to one, would win because the other horses had been interfered with. The horse did run and did win. Luke promised Lizzie that they would only take her share of the winnings and run away and get married. But Luke is the one who has run away, taking our money, and the winnings."

"How much did you lose?

"Our savings amounted to three hundred pounds. Luke would have won three thousand."

The earl gave a silent whistle.

"Poor Lizzie," said Emily suddenly, and with the perspicacity of the very drunk, she added, "Honour to marry a fisht footman. Great honour. Turned her head."

"Well, I hope this will be a lesson to all of you," said the earl heartlessly. "Next time put your savings in a safe place and don't trust scullery maids with the information."

"Very good, my lord," said Rainbird woodenly.

"Lizzie musht have money." Emily lurched to her feet and grabbed her reticule and began to fumble in it. "Money for Lizzie."

"We will attend to this matter later," said the earl crossly. "I shall see Charteris to-

morrow and find a direction for this footman. He might call to see his family."

But Emily had extracted a roll of notes
from her reticule and was carefully counting
them out. "Three hundred!" she said triumphantly. "Take it." She thrust the notes at
Rainbird.

"Oh, take the damned money and be off
with you," shouted the earl, losing his
temper. Here he was all ready to take his
love in his arms, and he was being thwarted
by servants' problems. Servants! How he
loathed them.

Rainbird took the money, bowed, and
scuttled off.

"Now," said the earl, pulling Emily towards him and beginning to undress her.

"What are you doing?" cried Emily, beat-
ing feebly at his efficient hands.

"Undressing you."

"Why?"

"To make love to you."

"Think of the king," muttered Emily.
"Think of the king."

But he began to kiss her. She swayed
drunkenly, feeling her senses reeling.

How he had managed finally to undress
himself as well as her during all those kisses
was a mystery to Emily. She wondered

194

vaguely whether it were a gentlemanly art, like fencing or boxing. His naked skin against her own fevered body felt beautifully cool.

She made one last heroic attempt to think of King George, and then wound her arms about her husband's naked back and floated off in a red mist of sensation. She cried out in alarm at the pain of losing her virginity, but then heard only his voice telling her how beautiful she was. At times Emily was able to wonder whether it was the amount she had drunk that was making the room reel or whether it was all the delicious kissing and caressing.

She finally floated off to sleep while the earl held her tightly, dizzy with gratitude for this naked, passionate wonder that was his new bride, and not knowing how very nearly King George had ruined his wedding night.

"So," said Rainbird grimly after the staff had finished their evening meal, "the money is back and there are to be no more rows and recriminations. We have all—understandably—been hard on Lizzie. That is, with the exception of Joseph. Why you, Joseph, were shouting and screaming and hitting the girl when *you* were the one who lost money before this on gambling, I fail to comprehend. Do eat something, Lizzie. I feel you have been punished enough. And, yes, I am sorry I soaped your mouth. Had I not been so rushed and busy, I would have taken the time to find out what was bothering you."

"Ungrateful, that's wot she is," said Joseph passionately. "Slut!"

"Joseph, I am warning you," said Rainbird, "that if you say one more hard word to Lizzie, I shall personally take you out and thrash you."

Joseph relapsed into silence but continued to growl at the pathetic, crushed figure that was Lizzie. That Lizzie could even *look* at another footman with him around was an outrage.

Lizzie found her voice at last. "Please, Mr. Rainbird, I want to go to church," she whispered.

Lizzie was Roman Catholic and went to church at St. Patrick's, Soho Square, unlike the rest of the servants, who belonged to the Church of England and infrequently attended services at the Grosvenor Chapel.

"Very well," sighed Rainbird. "But don't be too long."

Lizzie threw her shawl over her head and slipped out of the servants' hall.

"I don't know what come over our Lizzie," mourned Alice.

"She's a clever wee girl and better at her learning than the rest o' ye," said the cook. "Stands tae reason she gets fed up being treated like dirt."

"We don't treat her like dirt," said Jenny hotly.

"We pushed her around a bit wi' all the fuss o' the wedding breakfast, and me worse than any o' ye," said the cook regretfully. "The idea o' marrying a first footman is a big step up for her. Ah, well, it jist goes tae show what happens when the ladies don't keep tae their rightful stations in life."

"I hope nothing bad happens to our new countess," said Rainbird anxiously. "Soon she'll be leaving here and there will be nothing more we can do to protect her."

Lizzie scurried through the dark and windy streets. The rain had stopped, and ragged clouds scudded high above over the chimney tops.

She felt her disgrace keenly. How could she ever have imagined that a first footman would stoop low enough to marry her?

Joseph's cruelty was like salt in a wound. He had been worse than the rest.

During the wedding breakfast, Lizzie had been unable to bear the suspense any longer and had called at Lord Charteris' town house next door and had asked the butler, Blenkinsop, if she might speak to Luke.

"No, you might not," had said Blenkinsop awfully. "He rushed in here waving poundses and poundses and was most coarse and rude to me. Said he was going out of town on the next stage. Good riddance, I say." Lizzie had trembled and demanded to know which stage the footman had taken, but Blenkinsop had replied he neither knew nor cared. When she had returned to her own kitchen to be berated for leaving by a furious Angus, it had struck Lizzie that she had been gulled. Although she had tried to believe Luke would come back for her, she knew in her heart of hearts he would not. That was when she had broken down and confessed all.

Trying to blot out the memory of that humiliation, she hurried faster, and was relieved when she could leave the dark streets behind and plunge into the sanctuary of the church.

Lizzie trembled at the very idea of making her confession. Instead, she prayed long and hard for forgiveness and for a return of the humility that had once kept her cheerful and content.

At last, much comforted, she rose, feeling stiff, for she had been kneeling a long time, and made her way out, standing in the entrance to the church and adjusting her shawl about her head.

The rain had come on again and was drumming down on the muddy streets.

"Pardon me, miss," said a soft voice behind her. "May I take the liberty of offering you my escort? I have an umbrella."

Lizzie swung round. A neat, dapper man was standing behind her.

"I do not know you, sir," said Lizzie nervously.

"I shall introduce myself. Paul Gendreau at your service. Valet to milord, the Comte St. Bertin."

Lizzie bobbed a curtsy. "Lizzie O'Brien," she said shyly. "Scullery maid."

He nodded and began to crank open his umbrella with a gadget in the shaft.

"I give you good evening, sir," said Lizzie, "but I am perfectly well able to go home by myself."

"Not in this rain," he said calmly. He held the umbrella over their heads.

Lizzie glanced at his face. She could only see the gleam of white teeth and the shine of a pair of eyes.

The rain strengthened, glittering rods of water drumming on the cobbles of the square in front of them.

Lizzie gave a little sigh. Surely nothing worse than the treachery of Luke could happen to her again so soon.

She meekly fell into step beside her new friend.

# Chapter Eleven

*The cruellest lies are often told in silence.*
                    —Robert Louis Stevenson

The announcement of the earl and Emily's wedding appeared in *The Morning Post* the next morning.

The wedding couple was awakened by the noisy arrival of Mrs. Otterley. Her raucous voice rose and fell as she berated Rainbird and demanded to see her brother *immediately*.

Soon there came a scratching at the bedroom door, followed by Rainbird's apologetic voice explaining Mrs. Otterley was in the front parlour, waiting, and refused to leave.

The earl sighed and kissed Emily. "I shall get rid of her," he said. "Do you wish to rise and dress? Are you hungry?"

"Yes, Fleetwood," mumbled Emily, suddenly shy at the sight of his naked, muscled body as he climbed out of bed.

"I miss my valet," he said. "But there is no room here for extra servants."

"Will your sister be very angry?" asked Emily.

"Yes, but she will not be allowed to come near you."

After he had donned his small-clothes, he pulled on a damask banyan, that three-quarter-length easy coat which for two centuries now had been considered suitable for undress, thrust his feet into slippers, and made his way downstairs.

Emily got up, feeling languid and slightly unwell. She put on her night-gown and wrapper and went up to her old bedroom on the next floor, where most of her clothes were still kept.

Her husband's luggage and clothes were lying about the room. He had obviously decided to use the upstairs bedroom as a dressing-room.

Emily was taking a morning gown out of the wardrobe when she saw he had placed a pile of manuscript and letters on the desk. She walked over to the desk to check if it was still locked. It would be too awful if Fleetwood found the incriminating papers.

The desk was locked. She glanced idly

down at the manuscript and then felt herself go cold.

The name "Emilia" caught her eye. She turned over the pages with a sinking heart. It was quite obviously notes and a first draft of that wretched book. There could be no other explanation. Her husband, the Earl of Fleetwood, had written that horrible book. And yet he had married her, which proved he did not know the secret of her birth, and had not used her as a model for his Emilia.

But what if he ever found out? The contempt in that book for the upstart Emilia had been savage.

Emily sat down suddenly and buried her face in her hands.

Yesterday, her ambition to be a countess had been all that mattered. Now she only wanted his love, and the thought of losing that love was more terrifying than the thought of losing her title.

From downstairs rose the steady complaint of Mrs. Otterley's voice, punctuated by the masculine rumble of the earl's, and then Mrs. Otterley could be heard crying.

"I can't go on with this deception," thought Emily wildly. "I just can't. Can there be one slim hope he might forgive me?"

She washed and dressed. She heard the street door slam.

The earl climbed the stairs to their bed-chamber. There was a short silence and then Emily heard him ascending the next flight.

He came in and stood looking at her, his face grim.

"What is the matter, Fleetwood?" Emily faltered. "Is your sister so very angry?"

"Yes, but she has also brought bad news. Our brother Harry is dead. He died fighting bravely. And so comes the end of one of the most miserable chapters in my life."

He sat down and buried his head in his hands.

Emily looked at him helplessly. She shyly reached out and stroked his hair. He caught her hand and held it.

"I have to go to the War Office, my love," he said. "This is a grim start to our marriage."

"Do you wish me to accompany you?"

"No. Take the carriage and go to see your uncle. Stay there until I send for you. You will be besieged with callers today and I am sure you will wish to avoid them."

Outside Number 67, Mr. Percival Pardon waited patiently. He had called to present his compliments to the new countess and had been told, along with the other callers, that neither the earl nor the countess would be receiving guests that day.

But he was anxious to get a look at this beauty who had snared Fleetwood. Ever since he had read the announcement in the newspaper that morning, he had been consumed with curiosity. He was also anxious to ingratiate himself with the new countess. Mr. Pardon liked to be the fashion, and the only way he ever knew how to go about it was to attach himself to London's newest darling of the ton. Although Bessie and Harriet and their mothers might exclaim over poor Fleetwood having been "trapped" by a Nobody, Mr. Pardon knew the ways of the ton, and knew this countess was already the darling of society, as any woman who had managed to capture the handsome earl must be.

He was soon rewarded by the interesting sight of the earl leaving Number 67. The earl wore a black armband. Mr. Pardon remembered all that gossip about the death of the first Countess of Fleetwood. Surely Fleetwood had not killed his new bride so soon!

Rain smeared the carriage windows, and

he rubbed them impatiently with his sleeve. The day was cold and wet. The hot bricks at his feet had lost their warmth and he was just deciding to tell the hired coachman to move on when the door of Number 67 opened again and Emily came out.

Mr. Pardon stared and stared. She was standing on the step, drawing on her gloves and talking to the butler. Despite her fine clothes, he recognised her immediately. There could not be two such beauties in the whole of England. The new Countess of Fleetwood was that little chambermaid who had taken his fancy four years ago. The fact that Emily's "taking his fancy" had meant the girl had nearly been raped and that the butler who had defended her had suffered an apoplexy did not give Mr. Pardon one qualm.

In his opinion, pretty servant girls were there for the taking. Sometimes their masters and mistresses became all Methodist and ordered him from the house, but mostly they turned a blind eye to his amorous adventures. Unlike prostitutes, servant girls did not cost anything and were more likely to be free of disease.

He ordered his coachman to follow Emily's carriage.

While he was driven along, he turned his agile mind to the low state of his finances. He was sure the earl knew nothing of Emily's background. Wait a bit. In the north, she had been called Jenkins, and before her marriage she had been calling herself Goodenough!

Mr. Pardon sat back and smiled. This countess was an adventuress, and would no doubt pay heavily to have her secret kept.

Her carriage stopped outside a house in Park Lane. Mr. Pardon waited until she had gone inside, called his footman, who was standing on the backstrap, and told him to make discreet inquiries as to the name of the people occupying the house.

After about ten minutes, the footman came back. The house, he said, was occupied by the Countess of Fleetwood's uncle, Mr. Benjamin Goodenough.

"Her partner in crime," thought Mr. Pardon gleefully. "Now, if I present my card, I shall be left standing outside and then sent away. I know. I shall say that Mr. Goodenough is expecting me; don't bother to announce me, fellow, and walk in."

Rainbird, after seeing Emily off, walked down to the kitchen where Angus was bent over the fire, stirring something in a pot. The rest of the servants, even Dave, were abovestairs, putting the house to rights, and lighting fires in all the rooms, for the rain outside was changing to sleet.

"What a spring!" Rainbird shivered. "Well, our Lizzie was looking much more cheerful this morning."

"Aye," said Angus. "I think she's realised there's not been much damage done, now that my lady gave us the money."

"All the same," said Rainbird, "I hope Luke never comes near here again. She was badly hurt and shamefully tricked. But I tell you, Angus, just before she came down the stairs last night, I could swear I heard her talking to someone outside."

"Did you ask her if she was?"

"To tell the truth, I did not like to. She behaved badly over the taking of the money, but it made me realise she is not allowed any private life or dignity. But now I'm worried in case Luke came back last night and she is planning to run away with him."

"She wouldn't have looked so calm if that had been the case, said Angus. "She seemed quite happy last night and quite her old self this morning. The church always did Lizzie a power of good."

"Everything seems to be worrying me this morning," said Rainbird. "Must be the weather. I keep feeling I should have gone with my lady to check on the servants in Park Lane. The butler, Giles, is a regular fellow, but Mr. Goodenough is the kind of man other servants might take advantage of."

"Why don't ye run along then," said the cook impatiently, "and stop interrupting me at my work?"

Rainbird reached the house in Park Lane minutes after Mr. Pardon had made his entrance.

Giles let him in. "They've got company," he whispered. "Some fop said he was expected and pushed his way in. I feel something's wrong, for I heard my lady cry out. They have not rung for tea or wine or anything, so I don't know what's going on."

"Didn't he give a name?"

"Just said he was expected and walked in. He heard the voices from the drawing-room and went straight up there. But they haven't asked for him to be put out, so it must be all right."

"What did this fellow look like?"

"Oh, highly painted, weak sort of ferrety face, quite the dandy."

"I'll just go up and listen outside the drawing-room door," said Rainbird.

"You can't do that!" exclaimed Giles, but Rainbird was already on his way upstairs.

Rainbird pressed his ear to the panels of the green-and-gold drawing-room door.

". . . so you'd better pay up, my little servant, if you want me to keep quiet," he heard a mincing voice say.

"How much?" Rainbird heard Emily asking, her voice high and strained.

"Ten thousand pounds."

"We cannot afford such a sum!" Emily's voice again. Rainbird felt impatient with Mr. Goodenough. Why did he not stand up for her? Why was he letting her cope with this man on her own? But Mr. Goodenough had let Emily cope with most of the problems before her marriage, Rainbird remembered.

"You forget," came the nasty mincing voice again. "You told me, my dear countess, that you never stole any money from Sir Harry Jackson, that he left Spinks here the lot in his will. It was a fine house and lands. Ten thousand pounds is nothing to you."

"Mr. Pardon," Rainbird heard Emily say, "if I knew ten thousand pounds was *all* you were asking, I might be prepared to meet your terms. But when that money is gone, you will be back for more. And back. Such is always the way of blackmailers."

"So young and so wise to the world," mocked Mr. Pardon. "You have until tomorrow evening. I shall meet you here at six. If you do not give me the money, I shall go direct to Fleetwood."

"What's happening?" Rainbird swung round and saw Giles standing behind him.

"Nothing," said Rainbird hurriedly. Unlike the earl, Rainbird had no faith in the ability of his servants to keep their mouths shut. "I think I hear someone approaching the door," he said hurriedly. "You know Lord Fleetwood would send you packing if he found out you'd been eavesdropping on his wife's conversation." He went down the stairs, pulling Giles after him.

"Let me take that, Lizzie," cried Joseph, relieving the scullery maid of a heavy coal-scuttle. "You shouldn't ought to be carrying heavy things like that."

"Yes, and why don't you go downstairs

and have a bit of a rest," said Jenny. "You've done enough."

"I've still got the stairs to do," said Lizzie.

"Reckon I can do those," said Alice. "Run along, Lizzie."

"Yes, dear," said Mrs. Middleton, "we're nearly finished. I think these spring flowers add a nice touch of colour." She tweaked a daffodil into place in the flower arrangement she had been working on.

"You make me feel useless," said Lizzie. "I'd really rather be working . . . honestly."

They all exchanged glances and then looked at her anxiously.

"You can do the stairs then," said Alice. "But don't you go tiring yourself out."

Lizzie blinked back tears. She found their kindness made all her guilt come rushing back. Even Joseph had gone out of his way to be nice to her.

She took her cloths and brushes and went out to clean the stairs. As she worked her way steadily down from the attics, her thoughts kept returning to Paul Gendreau, the French valet who had escorted her home. When they had reached the more well-lit streets, she had been able to see his face clearly. It was a nice face, thought Lizzie, a bit sallow, but with a good firm jaw and mouth. Somehow, she had found herself telling him all about Luke and the money. The relief of unburdening herself to a sympathetic listener had greatly eased her heart, but now she wished she had not been so open. What did he think of her? He might think she was a stupid peasant who fell in love with every charlatan who showed an interest in her. She should not be thinking of him at all. Valets were a cut above first footmen—and only look where her vanity had already led her! And Joseph had become Joseph again—kind, teasing, and a bit silly. Dear Joseph.

Lizzie began to say her prayers as she cleaned each step, trying to shut out all worldly thoughts. She jumped as she heard the backstairs door in the hall slam. Rainbird shouted when he saw her, "Fetch everyone, Lizzie. Something terrible has happened!"

They all gathered round the table in the servants' hall. Rainbird stood at the head of the table and addressed them.

"My lady's secret has been found out," he said, "by a Mr. Percival Pardon. He recognised her. I think he remembers her from a time he visited Sir Harry Jackson. I did not tell you, my lady is not only of common stock, but once worked as a chambermaid. Mr. Goodenough was the butler in the same household—Sir Harry Jackson's. Sir Harry died and left his lands and fortune to Goodenough, then called Spinks, so they came by the money honestly, and changed their names legally. Now this Pardon is blackmailing my lady to the tune of ten thousand pounds."

"But cannot we tell my lord—cannot *she* tell my lord—the truth?" said Mrs. Middleton. "He is so much in love with her, he is bound to forgive her."

"It is well known that Lord Fleetwood detests the servant class," said Rainbird. "He might not forgive her. He does not know she is of common stock, either, for we—I—had that scrivener forge papers. We must save her. We must do something. She has been good to us, very good."

"What if my lord *did* kill his first wife?" said Jenny. "He'll kill this one if he finds out."

"He mustn't find out," said Rainbird. "What are we to do?"

"What kind o' man is this Pardon?" asked Angus MacGregor.

"I waited outside and followed him to see where he went. He is living in modest lodgings in Mount Street above a pastry cook's.

He is a fop; middle-aged, dissipated face, richly dressed."

"Not strong, I gather?" said Angus, stroking his chin.

"No, but not like to drop dead before tomorrow," said Rainbird tartly.

"Reckon we could threaten him," said Alice slowly.

They all looked at her impatiently. Slow and beautiful Alice was regarded by them all as being singularly addlepated.

"Garn," said little Dave. "We'd be arrested, sure as eggs is eggs."

Alice yawned and stretched. Then she said, "But he tried to blackmail a countess. If *he* talks, then *we* talk, and my lady and Mr. Goodenough have done nothing against the law—well, apart from them forged papers, and we can always burn them, for she changed her name right and proper and was married as Miss Goodenough and that was her legal name. So this Pardon chap ain't going to go hollering to the law. We kin all stick together and say as how we *all* heard him trying to get money out of my lady. All we got to do is to get him to come round here after my lord and lady have been served their dinner."

"But how do we do that?" asked Rainbird impatiently.

"By George!" exclaimed the cook. "We *kidnap* him—that's what."

Mrs. Middleton let out a faint scream. "We cannot *do* such a thing. Servants do not kidnap gentlemen."

"I think Alice has hit on it," said Rainbird slowly. "Never credited you with having ideas before, Alice."

Alice blushed. "Been thinkin' a lot about it," she admitted modestly. "Secrets always come out somehow. I mean I didn't know that someone would demand money from my lady, but I thought something would happen, and worry about her fair sharpened my brain-box."

"Now, let me see," said Rainbird. "We'll need a closed carriage, strong rope, and something to gag him with."

"What if he's gone out for the evening?" asked Lizzie.

"We'll wait until he comes back—even if it takes all night."

"But what if my lord and my lady wonder where the servants have gone?" demanded Mrs. Middleton.

"Well, you womenfolk won't be coming with us," said Rainbird. "They won't notice

216

as long as they've got someone to wait on them. They're too newly married to notice anything but each other."

"But my lord's brother has just died," said Lizzie doubtfully, "and you said Lord Fleetwood was very upset. He might not be feeling romantic enough not to notice."

"Mrs. Middleton will think of something to say," said Rainbird impatiently. "Now, let's work out our plan of battle. . . ."

The earl collected his bride from the house in Park Lane late in the afternoon. He accepted her explanation that Mr. Goodenough had gone to lie down, and being too taken up with distress over his brother's death, he failed to notice that Emily was unnaturally white and strained.

He went upstairs to change for dinner as soon as they arrived home—a process that took a whole hour, the earl finding it hard to master the intricacy of his cravats without the help of his valet. He then had to wait downstairs for his wife, Emily being still too shy to share a dressing room with him and having not yet moved her belongings into the back bedroom so that she might have a dressing room all to herself.

When they sat down to dinner, he talked

about what he had learned of his brother's funeral in Portugal. Emily noticed the strain and pain on his face and knew she was about to add to it. Percival Pardon would never keep that secret, of that she was sure. He would demand more and more money until she could not pay him further, and then he would talk.

Unaware that his bride was suffering the tortures of hell, the earl talked in a low voice about how good Harry had been when they had been boys together, before he, Harry, had turned out a wild, unmanageable rake.

By the time Alice and Jenny had cleared the covers and set down the port and walnuts, the earl finally noticed Emily's pallor.

"You must not take my family tragedy to heart," he said gently. "Harry's death is a mercy in a way. . . ."

"I must tell you something," said Emily, gripping the edge of the table so that her knuckles stood out white.

Mr. Percival Pardon was feeling pleased with the world. The blackmailing of Emily gave him a heady sensation of power. That would teach the little slut to repel his advances.

He finished his toilet by sticking a diamond pin in his stock, took his hat and cane and descended the stairs, and then stood on the pavement looking for a hack, and thinking that he would soon be able to afford a private carriage once more.

A closed carriage drew up beside him, the burly red-haired driver up on the box swathed in a greatcoat and shawls.

"Do you want a carriage, master?" called the driver. Mr. Pardon hesitated. The driver's accent had been Scotch, and although Mr. Pardon's country home was on the Scottish borders, he was suspicious of every member of that disgustingly independent race. But the carriage was well set up and rather above the usual standard of hackney carriage.

"Take me to Brooks's," he said.

He opened the carriage door and climbed in. There were two men and a boy inside. He opened his mouth to shout and a handkerchief was roughly shoved into it. Hands seized him, ropes bound him, and then, spluttering behind his gag with outrage, he felt himself being thrust into a sack.

# Chapter Twelve

*For herein may be seen noble chivalry, courtesy, humanity, friendliness, hardiness, love, friendship, cowardice, murder, hate, virtue and sin.*

— Sir Thomas Malory

"No," said the earl quietly, "I think what I have to tell you is more important."

"But, Fleetwood . . ."

"You must let me speak. I have been plucking up my courage to tell you this since my visit to the War Office."

"Go on," said Emily, although she wanted to scream at him that she had just screwed *her* courage up to the sticking-place and felt she would fail to say anything if she had to wait much longer.

But the earl's next words drove all thoughts of her own predicament out of her head.

"Harry killed Clarissa," said the earl flatly.

Emily looked at him in wonder. "I fear

220

I cannot have heard you aright. Did you say . . . ?"

"Yes. My brother killed my wife."

"But *why?*"

He signed "How can I even begin to describe Clarissa to you? Clarissa was very beautiful, very witty, very amusing. I was head over heels in love with her. But that love lasted only a few months after our marriage. She was a flirt. She demanded, not only all the attention, but was never happy unless she had some man desperately in love with her, ready to die for her. She had that power. Only I seemed to know her for what she was, callous and vain and greedy.

"She tormented one man and then another. In an attempt to remedy matters, I took her out of society, took her to my country estate, and told her she would never see London again until she learned to behave herself. I did not entertain. I knew the marriage was a failure and should have put an end to it, but my wretched pride kept telling me that I had made my marriage vows and must not break them. Then Harry came on a visit. He had to rusticate, he said, for the duns were after him. Harry was wild and heedless. But he was my brother and I thought even Clarissa would leave my brother alone.

"For a time, that appeared to be the case. They did not even seem to like each other. Harry began to become haggard and ill. I suggested we call a physician because I was becoming alarmed about him. He said I should not trouble my head over him because he was such a wastrel, he was not worth anyone's concern.

"I had ceased to have marital relations with my wife. I did not know, therefore, that she had been having an affair with my brother. They were so discreet, so circumspect, that even those gossipy servants of mine did not find out.

"But Clarissa began to tire of him, as she tired of all men once she had them firmly under her spell. She met him in the wood near my home and there told him she was finished with him. He refused to believe it. She had been promising to run off with him. She taunted him, saying he was only half a man and not good enough to keep such as herself amused. He raised the handle of his riding crop and threatened her. He was drunk, for guilt had made him come to drink too hard and too deep. He said he would strike her. She laughed and laughed and dared him to even try. He was mad with rage and grief and he struck her and struck her."

The earl fell silent. "And then?" prompted Emily shakily.

"I did not know any of this at the time. I thought she had been having an affair with one of the gamekeepers or one of the servants. At other times, I thought some vagrant had been wandering on the estate and had murdered her for her jewellery and had then panicked and fled without taking the jewels she wore.

"The day before her funeral Harry left without even waiting to say goodbye. I began to have an uneasy feeling about him, about his leaving so abruptly. I learned he had bought a captaincy in a regiment. That was odd because Harry always swore that men who went to fight were fools. He never wrote to me, but I heard of him from time to time, and last year one of his brother officers, home on leave, told me he had set sail for Portugal with Wellington's troops."

"How did you find out he committed the murder?" whispered Emily.

"The idiot left a sealed letter for me to be opened after his death. It is a miracle his commanding officer did not read it. I told my sister this day of what Harry had done. Now I have told you. I felt there should be no secrets between us."

"Oh, Fleetwood, you must be feeling wretched!"

"No, not really," said the earl with a sudden smile. "You see, I think I had come to know Harry had killed Clarissa. And Harry and I had grown very estranged, even before Clarissa's death. He was always in trouble. I must tell you the truth, and the truth is that the news of my brother's death has come as a blessed relief. Can you understand that?"

"I think so," said Emily.

"I must observe a certain period of mourning, nonetheless, but there is no reason for this tragedy to cast a shadow over our marriage."

Emily, head bowed, fiddled with her glass. "Now what have you to tell me?" he asked gently. "It can be nothing like as horrible as what I have just told you."

Emily looked up. She was almost inclined to lie so that she might make love with him, just one more night.

That autocratic, handsome face of his had become infinitely dear. But she knew if she did not tell him that evening, she might never find the courage again.

"I am being blackmailed," she said in a thin little voice.

"The deuce you are! Whom by? And why?"

"You are going to despise me, Fleetwood, but listen to me patiently and try to understand." Unable to look at him any longer, Emily addressed her wineglass.

In a tired, flat voice she told him everything, from her days as a chambermaid to her ambition to be a countess, from Rainbird's forgery to Percival Pardon's blackmail.

The earl looked as if a shutter had come down over his face. He watched her grimly as she fiddled with her glass and thought he could cheerfully kill her as poor Harry had killed Clarissa.

"I would have told you anyway," sighed Emily. "Even if I had not fallen so deeply in love with you, I would have told you, Fleetwood. That silly scullery maid was duped into stealing because she thought it would be a grand thing to marry a first footman. But at least she wasn't in love with him—or I am sure she was not. I will see lawyers and have you released from this marriage. I will—"

"Did you say you loved me?" interrupted the earl.

"Oh, yes, Fleetwood," said Emily miserably. "Very much."

"And you were a chambermaid?"

"Yes. And today I looked at your papers and came across a draft of that book, the one about the chambermaid, Emilia. Even if Pardon had not tried to blackmail me, that book alone would have forced me to tell you the truth. I know you despise servants."

"My darling," he said. "Do please look at me."

Emily raised her eyes.

He was regarding her with a mixture of tenderness, love, and exasperation.

"I could have strangled you when you said you wanted to be a countess. When you said you loved me, the sun shone once more on the dull landscape of my life."

"But I was a servant!" cried Emily.

"And now you are a countess," he said, beginning to laugh. "You wretched little liar, come and kiss me."

He stood up to meet her as she flew

round the table and caught her up in his arms.

He bent his mouth to hers, but before he could kiss her, a terrified scream of "Help!" came up from the bowels of the house like the voice of a soul crying out in hell.

"Curst servants," said the earl heartlessly, forgetting for the moment that he held an ex-member of that class in his arms.

"What a terrible cry," said Emily. "Oh, please find out what is going on."

"We will both descend to the lower regions, find out, and then go to bed," he said.

Putting his arm round his wife's waist, he led her down the back stairs.

As they approached the door to the servants' hall, they could not hear a sound. "Perhaps we imagined it," said Emily hopefully.

"Our hearts may beat as one, but not our imaginations," he said.

He pushed open the door. Emily peered over his arm.

Mr. Percival Pardon was bound to a chair. He was in an abject state of terror. The servants were standing round him. Mr. Pardon rolled frightened eyes in the earl's direction. "Fleetwood! Thank God.

You must remember me. Pardon. Percival Pardon. We met some years ago at the Dunsters," he said. "They are going to torture me. The red-haired one has gone to heat the poker on the kitchen fire."

"What an excellent idea," said the earl. "Come, my dear, and leave these good servants to their evening's fun and games."

"May I explain, my lord?" began Rainbird.

"Do not trouble," said the earl airily. "I am sure you have a perfectly reasonable explanation."

"Help me," bleated Mr. Pardon, tears standing out in his eyes.

"Fleetwood," said Emily desperately. "You must do something."

"Very well," said the earl, folding his arms. "You may proceed with your explanation, Rainbird."

Rainbird looked anxiously at Emily.

"He knows, Rainbird," said Emily.

"We weren't really going to torture him," said Rainbird. "Mr. Pardon here was blackmailing my lady and Mr. Goodenough to the tune of ten thousand pounds. He threatened to tell you my lady had once been a servant."

"And is this true, Pardon?"

"It is! It is!" cried Mr. Pardon. "But it was only my fun. I did not mean any harm. Let me go, Fleetwood, and I will never say a word."

"No, you won't," said the earl, "or your miserable life will not be worth living. Untie him, Rainbird."

Angus came in at that moment brandishing the poker, which looked as cold as indeed it was, the cook not having the heart actually to wave a red-hot poker over his victim in case he inadvertently burnt him.

He immediately started to poke the fire in the servants' hall, as if that was what he had meant to do all along.

As Mr. Pardon was untied and helped to his feet, the earl said, "I do not think I want to see your face in London for some time, Pardon. Make sure you leave Town by tomorrow morning at the latest."

Mr. Pardon babbled his thanks and stumbled out into the night by way of the area steps.

The earl walked forward and sat down at the servants' table, drew out a chair beside him, and motioned Emily to join him.

"Tell me, Rainbird," said the earl, "did you not think to ask *me* for help?"

"No, my lord," said the butler. "I could

hardly do that. It was my lady's place to tell you if she wished. Besides, your lordship's dislike of servants is well known."

"You are all rapidly changing my views. Your loyalty to my wife is commendable. I see now why she is become so attached to you all. You may all enter my staff, if you wish. I am a good employer and your wages will be of the best."

He looked curiously at their startled faces. What an odd lot they were, thought the earl, so different and yet so like a family. They seemed almost able to communicate with each other without opening their mouths.

"Thank you, my lord," said Rainbird, after looking around at the other servants. "But you forget. We are like to become independent by next year. We are going to buy a pub."

"Ah, that pub. Would you not all be tempted to continue in service? Perhaps your business might fail."

"We must take that chance," said Rainbird. "The girls must be free to marry, and we would all like to be our own masters."

"Then we shall patronise your pub when you are settled. Now, Rainbird, I gather you forged my wife's birth certificate. I will not feel at ease until we have formally been married again, although I am sure we have done nothing against the law as far as the actual marriage service is concerned. You are all invited, of course."

To his surprise, none of the servants looked in the least gratified. "It is a lot of work, Fleetwood," said Emily quietly, "not only to attend the wedding but once more to have to prepare the wedding breakfast. And we will have many more guests the next time, I should imagine."

"We will hire Gunter," said the earl expansively, meaning the caterers in Berkeley Square, "and my own servants will do the work. And you may order new liveries.

"Cen I have red plush with gold lacing?" asked Joseph eagerly.

"Anything you want," said the earl.

"And me, milor'," said Dave, his wizened little cockney face bobbing up at the earl's elbow. "Kin I be a page and carry my lady's train? Blue velvet would be orful nice."

"You'll look like an organ grinder's monkey," said the cook.

Dave's face fell, and Emily said quickly, "I should like you to carry my train and I think you would look handsome in blue."

Then Emily saw Lizzie looking at her

hopefully, and added, "And new dresses for the girls, and Mrs. Middleton will need something very fine if she is to be maid of honour again."

The earl was about to protest, to say that the days when his wife needed a mere housekeeper as a lady-in-waiting had gone, but the sheer joy and gratification on Mrs. Middleton's face made him stay silent.

Rainbird had gone out to his pantry, and he came in bearing two bottles of wine and glasses.

"We would be honoured, my lord," he said, "if you and my lady would join us in a glass of wine."

"We would love to," said Emily, answering for her husband, who frowned a little, for he was anxious to have his bride all to himself.

"Play us a tune, Joseph," said Rainbird.

Joseph got his mandolin. "Perhaps it would not be suitable to have music," said Emily. "My lord has just received news of his brother's death."

"You may play, Joseph," said the earl, deciding to humour his wife's desire for the company of these rented servants.

They all sat down round the table as Joseph began to play.

Rainbird stood up and made a short witty speech and then proposed a toast to the happy couple. Then Angus sang a mournful Scottish ballad, and Joseph followed that with a popular song. Rainbird did one of his juggling acts and the servants cheered.

The Earl of Fleetwood leaned back in his chair, all at once happy and relaxed.

Blenkinsop, the Charterises' butler, was making his way home to Number 65 next door after a convivial hour at The Running Footman. He heard the sounds of merriment from Number 67 and leaned over the area railing so as to get a look through the high barred window of the servants' hall.

"Well, I never!" he exclaimed as he saw Lord and Lady Fleetwood happily drinking with their servants. "Lords and ladies ought to know their places. Now Lord Charteris has never even set foot in *our* servants' hall." And shaking his powdered head with disapproval, he went in next door and down to his dark, gloomy servants' hall and tried to persuade himself he was lucky not to be a rented butler like poor Rainbird.

Three hours later—for after the servants' party he had gone to Park Lane to tell Mr. Goodenough his worries were over—the Earl

of Fleetwood drew his wife into his arms
and began to kiss her unresponsive lips.

"What is the matter, Emily?" he asked,
propping himself up on one elbow and looking down at her as she lay in the bed beside
him.

"Nothing, Fleetwood," said Emily miserably.

"I would like you to call me Peter, at
least when we are in bed."

"Nothing, Peter. I am tired, that is all."

"Then perhaps you would rather sleep?"

"Yes, Peter," said Emily in a small voice.

He turned his back on her and blew out
the candle.

Behind his back came the sound of a
small, strangled sob.

He lit the candle again from the rushlight
and turned and looked at his wife.

"What on earth is the matter?" he said
testily, for frustration was making him furious.

"I w-want to b-behave like a l-lady, but I
*can't!*" wailed Emily.

"What on earth are you talking about,
my widgeon?"

"Ladies are *never* passionate," said Emily,
covering her face with her hands.

"And where did you come by such a stupid idea?"

"I got it from your book and . . . and Mrs. Middleton."

"My, dearest love, I should think Mrs. Middleton is really a miss and a virgin as well. As far as my book is concerned, that was written by a bitter man with a very narrow view of life. You have made me grow up, Emily. Ladies *are* passionate, real ladies, ladies such as yourself of warmth and generosity."

Emily took her hands down from her face.

"So I will not give you a disgust of me, Fleetwood—I mean, Peter—if I respond to you?"

"You will give me a disgust of you if you do not!"

Emily buried her face on his chest. "I was becoming jealous of Clarissa, too," she mumbled.

"Why?"

"Well, you said she was witty and beautiful and fascinating and—"

"And as cold as charity. All she craved was attention and the power it gave her. I was very green when I married her. Oh, Emily, kiss me. You and only you can take me to heaven and back. . . ."

"I heard my lady scream!" cried Mrs. Middleton, starting to her feet.

"What is wrong?" cried Lizzie.

But the men laughed and Alice and Jenny blushed and even little Dave turned as red as fire and buried his nose in his glass.

"Terrible the way you can hear everything in this house," said Rainbird, drooping one eyelid in a wink. "Play us something, Joseph, and let's serenade the happy couple." Lizzie and Mrs. Middleton sat down together, united in their bewilderment. "There are some things I do not understand about men and women," whispered Mrs. Middleton, taking Lizzie's little work-roughened hand in her own.

"Me neither," said Lizzie. "But none of the others seems to be worrying, so we may as well enjoy the party."

# Epilogue

*Our soul is escaped even as a bird out of the snare of the fowler; the snare is broken, and we are delivered.*
—The Book of Common Prayer

Surely bad luck had finally left Number 67, thought Lizzie.

She and the other servants were seated at the end of the long table that had been hired for the day to fit down the length of the front and back parlours to seat the wedding guests.

True to his promise, the earl had summoned his own servants to wait on his guests and the staff of Number 67. Lizzie thought they all looked as grand as the guests. Joseph was resplendent in the finest livery he had ever owned and his voice had become so refined, he was practically unintelligible. Dave kept looking down at the blue velvet of his new suit of clothes and stroking his sleeve with one little hand when he thought no one was looking. Mrs. Middleton was very stately in white-and-scarlet merino and with three feathers in her hair. Jenny and Alice were wearing India Muslin gowns, Jenny in pale pink and Alice in celestial blue. Rainbird looked dapper in a claret-coloured coat and green-and-gold-striped waistcoat, and Angus MacGregor had risen to the sartorial heights of intricately starched and tied cravat and a coat of corbeau Bath superfine.

Lizzie glanced down complacently at her own gown. What scullery maid had ever been allowed to wear India muslin before? It was of a leaf-green colour with little white dots, and each dot was embroidered onto the material, not stamped, a luxury that had sent Lizzie quite faint with delight when she had first seen it.

The house had not really been unlucky, thought Lizzie, not for the servants. Everything always came out well for them.

She glanced at Joseph and then looked away. Joseph was getting a bit above himself, the honour of being served at the same table as the quality having gone to his head. The week before the wedding, Joseph had taken Lizzie out walking. As usual, he had talked a lot about himself, but he also talked about how they would get married as soon as they had their freedom. This declaration of intent would once have sent Lizzie into the seventh heaven, but instead it had now left her feeling strangely anxious and depressed. She could not forget Mr. Gendreau, the French valet who had walked her home from the church. And yet what did she know of him other than a pleasant face, not very clearly seen in the weak light of the parish lamps? He had not talked much himself, but he had listened very sympathetically, and Lizzie was not used to anyone listening to her for any length of time—certainly not Joseph.

Lizzie had not had any free time to go back to St. Patrick's. She looked at her gown again and wondered if Paul Gendreau would like it. But there was little point in seeking him out. Loyalty chained her to Joseph as surely as her servant status chained her to Number 67. She had never realised before that Joseph, along with the other servants, had come to take it for granted she would marry him. So even when she got her freedom, she would find herself in another sort of cage.

Her pleasure in her new dress was marred by her worries, by her odd feeling that she no longer belonged with the others.

Rainbird was worried about money, for Emily had agreed to leave Clarges Street that very day, right after the wedding breakfast, and travel with her lord to his country estate. That would mean the house would probably stand empty for the rest of the Season. And he could not expect tips from these grand wedding guests, for Giles and the staff of the house in Park Lane would pick up any tips that were going.

All the other servants were in high spirits, and Angus, the cook, enlivened with champagne, was even flirting mildly with Mrs. Middleton, who was turning quite pink with gratification.

The wedding breakfast was over at last and they all stood out on the street to say goodbye to the earl and countess. Mr. Goodenough was to travel with them.

Emily shook hands with them all and thanked them warmly, begging Rainbird to let her know when they had their pub so that she might be one of their first customers. The earl also thanked Rainbird and the others and then handed Rainbird a wash-leather bag. Fitz asked for permission to kiss the bride and begged Emily to find him a lady as pretty as herself. Mrs. Otterley gave Emily two fingers to shake, saw her brother's furious face, and offered Emily her whole hand instead.

To the servants' extreme annoyance, Giles and his staff took themselves off to follow the earl and the countess to the country, leaving the Clarges Street staff with all the mess to clean up. As they returned to the servants' hall for a rest and gossip before changing back into their working clothes, Rainbird tipped out the contents of the bag that the earl had given him. Two hundred golden guineas spilled across the table.

"We're free!" said Rainbird in an awed voice. "Free at last. We can buy a pub and give Palmer his quittance." They all cheered, but when the cheering had died away, Lizzie said quietly, "There's someone knocking on the door."

Rainbird darted up the stairs.

He swung open the door, prepared to see one of the wedding guests who had left something behind, and found himself confronting Jonas Palmer, the Duke of Pelham's agent.

"I want to see the tenants," growled Palmer.

"You're too late," said Rainbird. "You must be the only man in London not to have heard the news. Miss Emily married

241

the Earl of Fleetwood and she and Mr. Goodenough have just left for the country. Still, that shouldn't worry you, as she paid in advance. And now I have something to tell you. . . .

"And I have something to tell *you*," said Jonas Palmer, pushing past Rainbird and walking into the front parlour, where the remains of the wedding breakfast were spread out. He seized a decanter and poured himself a glass of port and drained it in one gulp. "That's better," he sighed. "Was there ever such a coil? You've got another tenant."

"We don't need another tenant," said Rainbird.

But Palmer was not listening to him.

"The Duke of Pelham has returned from the wars and is getting his town house in Grosvenor Square redecorated and he's coming to live here for the rest of the Season. It's a mercy that harpy, Goodenough, has left, although I would ha' liked the pleasure of turning her out. But don't you go mentioning anything about your wages to Pelham, see!"

"Why not?" demanded Rainbird. "We are disgracefully paid."

"Because if you so much as tell him what you are getting, I shall tell him how you was dismissed from Lord Trumpington's house-hold for seducing Lady Trumpington, and I shall tell him how that bishop caught that Joseph fellow stealing."

"I have told you and told you," said Rainbird grimly, "that we were both innocent of the crimes we were accused of."

"But the duke will listen to me, not you, and I'll go and get Trumpington to add his word."

Rainbird opened his mouth to tell Palmer that not one of them needed to stay at Number 67 a moment longer, and then the thought struck him that the Duke of Pelham knew nothing of their miserable wages. Palmer had probably been charging him higher ones and pocketing the difference. What a marvellous farewell to servitude it would be if Palmer could be exposed as a bully, cheat, and liar. They had the money for their pub; they would only need to wait another two months for their freedom.

"When can we expect his grace?" he asked smoothly.

"Next week," said Palmer curtly. "You're looking very fine for a rented butler."

"The Earl of Fleetwood invited us all as guests to his wedding."

Palmer thrust his beefy face towards

Rainbird. "Don't you go getting ideas above your station," he snarled. "Remember, you're only servants and I hold you all *here*." He clenched his fist.

"If you have quite finished," said Rainbird icily, "I suggest you leave us to go about our duties."

Palmer eyed the remains of the meal greedily. But he was worried to death the duke might demand to see the estate books immediately, and Palmer wanted to go over them again to make sure there were no mistakes. He had not seen the duke for many years, having received all communications from him by letter. He remembered him as a slim, rather pretty youth. Should be no trouble there, but it would be as well to make sure.

He took himself off and Rainbird returned to the servants' hall with the news. Angus, Joseph, and even Dave were delighted at the thought of a possibility of unmasking Palmer. But the women were afraid. What could they, as mere servants, do to unseat the all-powerful Palmer? A duke's agent held more sway over the underlings than a country squire.

But as they talked and planned, even they began to brighten. They turned over their past successes, and comforted themselves with the thought that Palmer could really do nothing to them now. A servant with a bad reputation that was broadcast over London by a duke's agent could never hope to find another job; ladies and gentlemen of property, such as they were about to become, could not be harmed.

At last Rainbird reminded them, they were, for the time being, still servants. They changed back into their working clothes and set about their duties, each one of them wondering what the Duke of Pelham would be like.

A few days later, the Countess of Fleetwood stretched lazily in bed and rested her head on her husband's naked shoulder.

"I fear you are not a very conscientious landowner, Peter," she murmured. "We seem to spend most of our time in bed."

"Best place in the world," he said sleepily. "You are wonderful, my love, a real countess. One would think you had been born to the position."

"Did you expect me to behave like a servant?"

"No. But I am pleased the way you have

taken over the running of my household without depending on your private army."

"What army?"

"Those Clarges Street servants."

Emily laughed. "At least they changed your attitude towards the class of servants."

"Not quite. They are not proper servants. Perhaps there is something odd about that house after all. Perhaps the house has turned them into a small, highly intelligent force."

"Perhaps," said Emily with a yawn. "I, my love, am going to set you a good example by getting up." She threw back the covers and swung her legs over the side of the bed.

The earl sat up, reached over, and put his hands on her naked breasts and began to kiss the back of her neck.

"Oh, Peter," sighed Emily, leaning luxuriously back against him. "I fear, in some respects, I am not a lady at all!"

## DATE DUE